Much

by

Kathi Daley

This book is a work of fiction. Names, characters, places, and incidents either are products of the author's imagination or are used fictitiously. Any resemblance to actual events or locales or persons, living or dead, is entirely coincidental.

Version 1.0

This book is dedicated to Randy Ladenheim-Gil for not only being the best editor in the world but for putting up with my wacky schedule and always coming through.

I also want to thank the very talented Jessica Fischer for the cover art.

I so appreciate Bruce Curran, who is always ready and willing to answer my cyber questions.

Special thanks to Joyce Aiken, Nancy Farris, Vivian Shane, Robin Coxon, Marie Rice, and Janel Flynn for their contribution of recipes.

And, of course, thanks to the readers and bloggers in my life who make doing what I do possible.

And finally I want to thank my sister Christy for always lending an ear and my husband Ken for allowing me time to write by taking care of everything else.

Books by Kathi Daley

Come for the murder, stay for the romance.

Buy them on Amazon today.

Zoe Donovan Cozy Mystery:
Halloween Hijinks
The Trouble With Turkeys
Christmas Crazy
Cupid's Curse
Big Bunny Bump-off
Beach Blanket Barbie
Maui Madness
Derby Divas
Haunted Hamlet
Turkeys, Tuxes, and Tabbies
Christmas Cozy
Alaskan Alliance
Matrimony Meltdown
Soul Surrender
Heavenly Honeymoon
Hopscotch Homicide
Ghostly Graveyard - *October 2015*
Santa Sleuth - *December 2015*

Paradise Lake Cozy Mystery:
Pumpkins in Paradise
Snowmen in Paradise
Bikinis in Paradise
Christmas in Paradise
Puppies in Paradise
Halloween in Paradise – *August 2015*

Whales and Tails Cozy Mystery:
Romeow and Juliet
The Mad Catter
Grimm's Furry Tail
Much Ado About Felines
Legend of Tabby Hollow – *September 2015*
Cat of Christmas Past – *November 2015*

Seacliff High Mystery:
The Secret
The Curse
The Relic
The Conspiracy – *October 2015*

Road to Christmas Romance:
Road to Christmas Past

Chapter 1

Saturday, September 19

I watched as the black and white cat strolled up to the ferry dock. As he had every Saturday since Tara and I had opened Coffee Cat Books, the cat jumped up onto the bench in the viewing area and waited for the eleven o'clock ferry from the mainland to arrive. And as he had every Saturday for the same six weeks, a tall, elderly man wearing a black suit, a white shirt, dark glasses, and a black hat, disembarked and walked up the ramp toward the main street of Pelican Bay.

Now, it isn't at all odd for tourists to take the ferry from the mainland to Madrona Island. Every weekend hundreds of people travel to the touristy town on the south end of the island to enjoy the eclectic shops, fine dining, and island atmosphere. What is odd is that every Saturday for the past six weeks, the cat has jumped off the bench and followed that man, who then returns to the ferry for the trip east just three hours later.

I need to point out that my best friend and business partner Tara O'Brian and I only began noticing the man in the dark suit six weeks ago because that's when we opened our store. For all we knew, the man could have been arriving on the island on the eleven o'clock ferry on Saturdays for months, or even years.

"Our mysterious stranger is back," I said to Tara, who was preparing the coffee bar for the ferry passengers we knew would pile in for a beverage before heading into town.

"Is the cat there as well?"

"He is," I verified as I stacked the last of the new paperbacks I'd been organizing in the display window. "It's so odd the way the cat waits for the man and then follows him into town, even though I've never once seen him so much as acknowledge the presence of the animal."

"It's actually kind of creepy the way he looks directly ahead and never seems to notice anyone or anything around him. He didn't even stop to look at the pod of whales that were in the harbor when the ferry docked last Saturday."

Tara joined me at the window and we both watched the man walk past the shop.

"The way he walks with such purpose reminds me of a person who's sleepwalking or in a trance," I offered. "You know, he actually walks like a zombie. Maybe he *is* a zombie."

"He's not a zombie."

"He's really pale," I pointed out.

"He's not a zombie."

"And those clothes. So dated."

"Not a zombie."

"If it walks like a duck and talks like a duck . . ." I argued.

"There are no such things as zombies. Still, I do wonder where he goes every Saturday."

"I don't know, but I have to admit to being curious. Maybe one of us should follow him," I suggested. "From a distance of course, so as not to be conspicuous."

"The problem is that eleven o'clock on Saturday is one of our busiest times," Tara reminded me. "If one of us leaves to follow the man the one who stays will be swamped with the fifty people who are heading our way."

"Don't worry. I'd hurry," I assured Tara.

"Cait," Tara warned.

"Oh, okay. I'll stay."

The next thirty minutes were busy as passengers from the mainland filed in to order hot beverages. Tara's idea of including a coffee bar as part of the bookstore was a good one. I'm certain we wouldn't have half the business we do if folks from the ferry didn't wander into the shop in search of a latte and leave with a bagful of books and novelty items as well.

Tara set the drinks she had been making in front of me so I could ring them up. "One black coffee, one soy pumpkin latte, one chai tea with milk, and three cranberry muffins," I called out the order for two of our regulars, twin sisters Karla and Kayla Evington.

Karla and Kayla had grown up living in a two-story house a few doors down from the one where I grew up in the fishing village of Harthaven, the oldest settlement on Madrona Island.

"Thanks, Cait," Kayla said as she handed me a twenty-dollar bill. "This is my boyfriend, Kyle."

Kyle, Kayla, and Karla? Oh, no, that's not confusing.

"Kyle, this is Caitlin Hart. Her mom lives just down the street from my mom," Kayla introduced me to a tall, dark-haired boy who appeared to be about her age. "Cait was in high school when Karla and I were in grade school, so she used to babysit for us."

"I'm happy to meet you," I said.

"Your store is dope."

"Thank you." I smiled at the teenage boy with bangs in his eyes and shorts that sagged halfway down his butt.

"How is the new apartment working out?" I asked Kayla.

Karla and Kayla had graduated high school the previous spring and recently moved into an apartment not far from the bookstore.

"It's the bomb." Kayla grinned. "And the rental company changed their mind and decided to allow us to adopt the girls if we were willing to put down an additional deposit."

Karla and Kayla had their hearts set on adopting sisters, Sugar and Spice. The sisters had started off as feral kittens, but my Aunt Maggie had rescued them when they were very young and had been housing them in Harthaven Cat Sanctuary ever since. After several months of socialization with other cats and people, we'd decided they were ready for forever homes.

"And are you able to swing the deposit?" I asked.

"We are." Kayla grinned. "When can we pick them up?"

"I'll be here until five and Aunt Maggie is working at the Bait and Stitch today, but I could meet you at the cat sanctuary as soon as I get off if you'd like."

"We'd like," Karla chimed in as she picked up her pink to-go cup.

"Okay, I'll see you out at Whale Watch Point at about five fifteen. I'm glad it worked out for you to have the kittens."

The girls bounced away to drink their beverages and visit with the cats we were featuring that day. Coffee Cat Books is a unique endeavor Tara and I came up with one winter night as we sat in the oceanfront cabin I live in and dreamed about the *what ifs* in life. What if money was no object? What if talent wasn't a limitation? What if we could do anything we imagined we could do?

The enterprise became a reality the previous summer, when we were able to purchase the old fish cannery located on the wharf where the ferry currently docks. Tara and I had always dreamed of opening a bookstore with a coffee bar, but after Aunt Maggie founded the sanctuary, we came up with the idea of incorporating a cat lounge, where visitors to our shop could visit with animals that were currently available for adoption while reading the book they'd just purchased and sipping one of Tara's famous lattes.

We really did have the ultimate location. Right on the harbor, the bookstore was surrounded on three sides by beautiful blue water that complemented the green hillsides of neighboring islands in the distance. During the warmer summer months, the orcas that lived in the area came into the harbor to entertain customers who were lucky enough to be sitting on the wharf when they came by.

Although the whales were obviously a big draw, the store was designed to possess year-round appeal. While patrons could sit outdoors at the tables we'd provided during the summer, during the winter they could curl up on comfy sofas to read near the large stone fireplace that dominated one wall.

So far our plan to provide an enticing setting had worked, and we've been busier than we'd ever imagined. From my perspective, this is both a positive and a negative. I'm thrilled that we've been able to not only meet our financial obligations but also put some money away for the winter, but both Tara and I have been working a lot more hours than either of us will be able to maintain in the long run.

"Excuse me, miss." A tall, thin woman with a beaklike nose stopped me as I headed toward the cash register. " I was told the local newspaper had reopened. Do you have any copies of the most recent issue?"

"Actually, we sold out shortly after we opened this morning. The weekend issue has been selling faster than anyone can keep it in stock, but you might be able to pick up a copy at the newspaper office, which isn't too far a walk from here."

"What's so special about the weekend issue?" the woman asked.

"The cover story is about the body that was found in Roxi Pettigrew's burial site."

The woman frowned. "There were two bodies in one grave?"

"No, just one."

"Which one?" the woman asked.

"Roxi Pettigrew."

The woman's brow furrowed. "So Roxi Pettigrew's body was found in Roxi Pettigrew's burial site?"

"Yes."

"And this is front-page news?"

"It is when as of eight days ago Roxi was very much alive," I answered.

The woman was clearly confused.

"Roxi's husband, Jimmy, passed three months ago as a result of an automobile accident. She buried him in the Madrona Island Cemetery and purchased the plot next to his for her own eventual demise so they could spend eternity side by side. Five days ago her best friend, Stacy, reported that Roxi seemed to be missing; she'd missed church on Sunday and failed to show up for work on Monday. Stacy went by Roxi's apartment and it appeared her friend hadn't been there for a couple of days. Three days later, on Thursday evening, the lawn service that tends to the cemetery on a weekly basis noticed that the sod covering Roxi's gravesite appeared to have been disturbed. Yesterday they removed the sod and dug up the grave and Roxi was found buried inside. The story was reported in this morning's newspaper and, like I said, the issue has been flying off the racks ever since."

"So how did Roxi end up in her grave?" The woman was intrigued.

"That's the thing: No one knows who killed her or how she got there. All we know for certain is that Roxi showed up for her shift as a waitress at the Driftwood Café on Thursday, September tenth, and attended the weekly meeting of the Mystery Lovers Book Club that evening. The owner of the Driftwood Café confirmed that Roxi worked Monday through Thursday and wasn't expected to work over the weekend. Stacy confirmed that the mail that was delivered to Roxi on Friday, the eleventh, was picked up, opened, and sitting on her kitchen table, so she assumes Roxi was home on Friday morning. The weekend edition of the *Madrona Island News* was delivered on Saturday morning but was never picked up from her doormat, so we're assuming something happened to her between the time the mail was picked up on Friday and the newspaper was delivered on Saturday. It's possible whatever happened to Roxi happened at some point after Saturday, though, because Stacy didn't know what Roxi planned to do on Saturday. Given the fact that she's been going out a lot, it's possible she had a date on Friday night and decided to stay over. She really wasn't due to be anywhere until church services on Sunday."

"Wow, it looks like you have quite a mystery on your hands."

"Unfortunately, we've had a rash of mysteries on the island as of late. You can find the weekend issue of the paper online if you're interested in following the story." I handed the woman a flyer that gave the Web site's address.

"Thank you. I'll look it up. I find myself very much interested to see how this whole thing turns out."

"Yeah, me too," I agreed.

After the woman walked away I decided to start unpacking the inventory that had come over on the morning ferry. In addition to the pink mugs with the Coffee Cat Books logo Tara and I had designed to use in the coffee shop and to sell in the bookstore, there were bookmarks, reading lights, and Coffee Cat Books T-shirts. There was also the weekly delivery of paperbacks to check in and set out.

There are tasks associated with owning a bookstore that I enjoy, like digging through the shipments we receive, and there are others that I don't, like the endless dusting required to keep our space clean and appealing. Tara handled most of the *real* work that was required of us as business owners. Not only did she take responsibility for ordering and controlling the inventory but she handled all the bookkeeping, as well as the daily task of baking the pastries we sell. I did want to be a contributing partner, so I tried to pitch in with dusting shelves, waiting tables, stocking inventory, and washing coffee mugs as often as I could.

"Where do you want these book bags?" I asked her.

"Why don't you arrange one of each design in the display window and then hang the rest on the rack near the coffee mugs?"

I grabbed an assortment of the colorful totes and headed toward the front window.

The wharf was littered with people enjoying the sunshine and mild temperature. One of the things I liked best about spending time in the bookstore was the festive atmosphere that accompanied our everyday life. There's something about the sounds and smells that accompany life on the ocean that can't be duplicated anywhere else.

Although, as with most things in life, with the beautiful comes the annoying. I cringed as a seagull swooped down and tried to steal one of Tara's muffins right out of a young girl's hand. We'd posted signs warning people not to feed the birds, but more often than not visitors to the island ignored the signs, and the birds had grown accustomed to regular snacks of the human variety.

"The lady in the red sweatshirt is interested in adopting Cleo," Tara informed me as I finished displaying the book bags and began tagging the shipment of T-shirts.

"Has she filled out an application?" I asked.

"Not yet. I thought you could help her with that while I restock the coffee bar for the next wave of customers."

"I'd be happy to."

While featuring the cats in the cat lounge hadn't eliminated the need to attend adoption clinics on the mainland, it had reduced the need to make the trip from two times per month to one. As word of the cat lounge spread, we hoped prospective families from the mainland would make the trip out to the island to meet the cats and buy a book.

"I understand you're interested in adopting Cleo," I said to the woman who was holding the white cat to her chest.

"I am. She's just the sweetest thing."

"All of our cats have been spayed or neutered. They're all current on their shots and have been checked out by our veterinarian. We have cat carriers for sale if you decide to take Cleo with you. I have applications if you'd like to fill one out."

"I'd like that very much."

Based on the loud purring, Cleo seemed as happy with the woman as she seemed to be with her.

"Did you come over on the eleven o'clock ferry?" I wondered.

"I live here. I moved to the island about a year ago, but I guess we haven't had the occasion to meet. My name is Trish."

"And I'm Caitlin Hart."

"You're the girl who solved all those murders. I'm happy to finally meet you. I heard about Roxi. Will you be investigating her murder as well?"

"I'm not really sure. I guess it depends how things develop."

"It's so odd that she ended up in her own grave, but I'm not surprised someone offed her."

"You knew Roxi?" I asked.

"We had some friends in common and tended to end up at many of the same social events."

"So why do you think someone would kill her?"

"I guess you've heard that she'd been partying a lot since her husband died."

"Yeah, I'd heard." Jimmy was friends with my brother Danny, and Danny was pretty tight with Roxi as well.

"My brother Danny mentioned that Roxi had been taking Jimmy's death pretty hard. I guess I don't blame her for wanting to go out rather than staying home all alone on the boat she lived on with Jimmy," I added.

"I don't disagree. The problem was that she wasn't just partying. She'd been flirting with pretty much the entire male population of Madrona Island, including other people's husbands. I know of three or four women in particular who are thrilled she's no longer a threat to their marriages."

"Really? Danny didn't mention that."

"I know who Danny is. He's the babe who owns the whale watch boat."

"Yes. *Hart of the Sea*."

"Danny seems like a nice guy, but he *is* a guy. Guys don't see flirting as a threat the way women do. There's a rumor that Roxi actually slept with a few of the married men who hung out at O'Malley's."

"Like who?"

"Griff Poolman for one. Trace Wood for another."

I knew both Griff and Trace and I found it hard to believe that either of them would cheat on their wives, but Roxi was extremely attractive. She had a certain way about her that let men know she was interested and available, and I could remember the trouble she'd created before she met Jimmy and he'd stolen her heart.

Trish completed her application, which looked to be in order, so I crated Cleo and sent the pair on their way. I checked on the remaining cats and then headed over to the coffee bar, where Tara was wiping things down. The crowd that had been mingling around had cleared out, which gave us a brief respite until the next ferry arrived.

"There's a stack of flyers for the Harvest Festival and Masquerade Ball on the shelf near the cash register," Tara informed me. "Be sure to hand them out to everyone who comes in. The committee is hoping for a good turnout this year."

Every year for as long as I can remember, the citizens of Madrona Island have thrown a huge Harvest Festival the last weekend in September. The highlight of the weekend is the formal Masquerade Ball, which is held in the old Waverly mansion, which is situated on the northeast side of the island, sitting on a huge estate located right on the water. Prior to the death of Cherise Waverly, the mansion had been a private home, but Cherise had died without children, so she'd donated the estate to the historical society.

The Madrona Island historical society is made up of a group of four senior citizens, including my Aunt Maggie, who manage the handful of historical buildings on the island. The other properties are insignificant; it's the mansion that gives the committee a reason to exist. The funds raised by the ball are used to maintain the property.

"Are you going with anyone?" I asked Tara.

Tara's love life has been unstable and fragile as of late. I know she has a crush on Danny, but I also know they've agreed that their lifelong friendship is too important to risk with a potentially messy love affair. Although I've witnessed a deeper level of caring between them lately, both seem content at the moment to pursue other people.

"I'm undecided at the moment," Tara shared. "I thought about asking Carl, but he seems to be intent on moving our relationship to a more serious level and I'm not sure I'm ready for that. I might end up volunteering to help with the food. If I'm busy serving it won't seem strange to attend alone. Are you going with Cody?"

Cody West and I have a relationship of indeterminate status. Cody was Danny's best friend when we were growing up. Like many little sisters, I used to tag along with Danny and his friends, and like many big brothers, Danny complained about it to no end. Cody, however, was always nice to me, which was most likely why I developed a huge crush on him the moment I hit puberty. When I was sixteen Danny and Cody graduated high school. While Danny planned to remain on the island, Cody had enlisted in the Navy. In a rash act that can only be attributed to teenage insanity, I decided to seduce Cody on the evening of his graduation in an effort to convince him to stay. My grand plan worked surprisingly well and we'd shared a magical night. The problem was that instead of staying, as I'd hoped, Cody left as planned, and I didn't see him again until he returned to the island a few months ago.

In the past few months Cody and I have spent a lot of time together. We worked side by side to solve three murders as well as a decades' old mystery. After retiring from the Navy he bought the *Madrona Island News* and has been working to bring the archaic newspaper into the twenty-first century. I can say with confidence that Cody and I have renewed our friendship, and any weirdness that might have occurred due to our one night of passion has been relegated to the distant recesses of my mind. What is unclear, though, is whether a relationship beyond friendship is in our future. I still have feelings for him, and it seems like he has feelings for me, but like

Danny and Tara, we both seem unwilling to risk what we have for the uncertainty of what might be.

"We haven't talked about it. I know he's superbusy right now with the reopening of the paper and the story about Roxi to stay on top of."

"If I didn't know Cody better I'd say he was the one who put Roxi in that grave," Tara teased. "Talk about a sensational story to get his newspaper up and running right out of the gate."

"Yeah, he's been swamped. He totally sold out of the first run of the weekend edition and is printing a second run this morning. He said he'd bring some copies by when they're ready. When I spoke to him earlier he asked if we could all get together this evening. He really wants to dig up some new clues so he has material for the Tuesday edition."

Somehow Cody, Danny, Tara, and I have morphed into the Scooby Gang when it comes to mystery solving on Madrona Island.

"He said he'd bring dinner," I added.

Tara shrugged. "I'm not busy."

"Do you think the mystery man from the ferry has anything to do with Roxi's death?" I asked.

"I don't see how."

"It's just that the guy is so odd and sort of creepy. And what is up with the cat? I mean, how does the cat even know it's Saturday? I've never seen it in the area, or anywhere else for that matter, on any day other than Saturday. Have you?"

"No," Tara admitted. "I can't say I've ever run into that particular cat on any other day. Maybe he's just well-trained. Perhaps he has an owner who tells the cat it's time to go to the ferry and he goes."

"Maybe." I was skeptical. Cats weren't normally all that trainable, but I had worked with a few really spectacular ones of late.

"Oh, look, here he comes," I said as the zombie stranger walked past the bookstore on his way back to the ferry.

As he had every other Saturday, the black and white cat followed him to the ferry terminal. When the man reached the loading area for walk-on passengers, the cat stopped and watched him board.

"That has to be the strangest thing I've ever seen," I commented as Tara joined me near the huge picture window that looked out over the wharf and the bay.

"Yeah, it is odd, but I'm sure there's a very simple explanation."

"Like what?" I asked.

Tara shrugged. "Maybe the guy comes to the island once a week to get a haircut or to visit a relative. Maybe he has a pocket full of cat treats, so the cat has gotten used to meeting him here. There could be any one of a dozen different explanations. What I do know is that we don't have time to worry about a mystery that most likely isn't even a mystery. We have this store to run."

"Yeah, you're right. What do you need me to do?"

"I have three orders that need to be delivered at some point today."

Tara nodded toward the counter, where there were three bags filled with special-order books.

"I'll take them," I offered. "Who are they for?"

"Bella and Tansy, Summer, and Marley."

Bella and Tansy are intuits—some say witches—who live in Pelican Bay and own Herbalities, a shop that sells herbs and herb products as well as offering fortune-telling services. While neither Bella nor Tansy will confirm or deny their witchy status, I've seen enough to know that those who believe in their magical powers aren't as far off base as one might think.

Summer is one half of the hippie couple known as Banjo and Summer. The eclectic pair lives in a hut on the beach and owns and operates a popular store called Ship Wrecked.

Marley Donnelly is my Aunt Maggie's best friend and business partner. Together, they own the Bait and Stitch, a unique store that sells fishing and sewing supplies.

"I'll go now; that way I should have plenty of time to make the deliveries and get back to help you with the last ferry of the day," I offered.

Chapter 2

I hung up my apron, grabbed the books, and headed out the door and down the street. It looked like there was rain on the horizon, so I decided it might be prudent to hurry to complete my task before the clouds that were heading our way arrived. Not that I was complaining about the rain. We did need a steady source of natural moisture to keep our forests green and our freshwater ponds and lakes filled.

The first shop I came to on my route was Herbalities. The store was empty of customers, which was odd for this time of the day on a Saturday. Like many of the shops on the island, Herbalities was closed on Sundays, making Saturday the only weekend day that visitors from the mainland could come in to buy the teas and medicinal tonics and lotions that made the enterprise so successful.

The first thing you noticed when you entered the shop Bella and Tansy owned was that it smelled like heaven. The herbs that were used in their teas and herbal remedies were displayed in jars that were strategically placed around the main room. In addition, bunches of freshly picked or dried plants were hung from the ceiling to provide added atmosphere.

"Caitlin, how nice to see you," Bella greeted me as I felt the stress of the day melt away. There was something about the serene aura of these women that made it almost impossible to hold on to any negative energy you might have brought with you when you entered their shop.

"I brought the books you and Tansy ordered." I set the pink bag with the Coffee Cat Books logo on the counter.

"How nice of you to deliver them. Tansy said you'd be by today to ask about Roxi Pettigrew."

"She did?" Even I didn't know I intended to ask about Roxi. "Is she here?"

"Actually, she isn't. Before she left, though, she asked me to inform you that Beatrice will be by to help."

"Beatrice? Who's Beatrice?"

Bella shrugged, but I was willing to bet she knew.

If recent history was an indicator, Beatrice would be a cat with witchy ways who would become a temporary part of my life.

"When will Tansy be back?" I asked.

"She's away on retreat, so it's hard to say exactly, but I'm sure she'll be back when it's time."

"Time for what?" I asked.

"I'm afraid I really don't know. Tansy did want me to give you this." Bella handed me a salve made of a mixture of herbs and other natural substances. "It's for your shoulder."

"But my shoulder is fine," I responded.

Bella just smiled.

"How did those herbs I sent over for Maggie work out?"

My Aunt Maggie had been exposed to arsenic over the past winter and, although it had worked its way out of her system, she still didn't feel quite like her old self, so Bella often sent herbs over to help increase her energy level.

"They seem to have worked like a charm. Aunt Maggie told me just the other day that she felt better than she had in years."

"I'm glad to hear that. I've been meaning to pay Maggie a visit, but first I was away at the yoga retreat and now Tansy is, so I'm handling the store on my own."

"When exactly did Tansy leave?" I wondered.

Bella shrugged. "A few days ago. I guess it must have been Tuesday."

"And she told you that I would be by today to ask about Roxi Pettigrew before she left?" I verified.

"Yes. Just as she was stepping onto the ferry."

"Roxi Pettigrew's body wasn't found until yesterday," I pointed out.

"Yes, I'd heard that. Is there anything else I can help you with?"

"I don't suppose you might be able to offer any insight as to how Roxi ended up in her grave?"

Bella winked at me but didn't answer.

I thanked her for the salve and exited the shop. The sky had continued to darken and the wind had picked up just a bit while I was speaking to Bella. Storms on the island tend to blow in and out on a regular basis, but for some reason I had a bad feeling about this particular one. Was it a portent? Probably not. While Bella and Tansy seemed tuned into the subtle vibrations of the universe, I was barely able to keep up with the clues that hit me smack-dab in the face.

Deep in thought, I headed next door to Ship Wreck, the shop owned by the hippie couple, Banjo and Summer. The hut in which they lived sat on one of the most beautiful beaches in the area. Although they didn't possess many modern conveniences, they seemed more content than anyone I'd ever met. Their shop carried a little bit of everything, from driftwood sculptures to homemade pottery to tie-dyed T-shirts. The sign on their door indicated that they were "open when they were open and shut when they were shut," and that was exactly the hours they kept: random and unpredictable.

"Afternoon, Banjo," I said as I walked in the front door. "I brought the books Summer ordered."

"She's not here right now, but I'll be sure she gets them. How's the new business going?"

"Really well. I'm glad we managed to get open during the summer. I feel like it gave us a running start going into winter. I guess you heard they'll be cutting back on the ferry schedule."

"Yeah, I heard. I guess it makes sense. We don't get a lot of foot traffic during the week once the summer crowds are gone. Of course Summer and I are looking forward to the slower pace of winter. We've barely had a minute to catch up on our soaps or help Cody with his remodel."

Banjo and Summer lived just down the beach from Maggie's neighbor, Mr.

Parsons. The free-spirited couple didn't own a television, so they tended to hang out with him to watch the old soap operas he had on tape. Cody had moved in to the third story of Mr. Parsons's house after he moved back to the island and was in the middle of remodeling the space to meet his needs.

"Cody will probably be busy working on the Roxi Pettigrew story for a while," I commented.

"Yeah, it's an odd one all right. Gotta admire the ingenuity of the killer. Who would ever think to look in someone's grave for their body? If the killer had done a better job replacing the sod I bet no one would ever have known what became of the woman."

"I guess we can rule out professional gardeners."

"I'm not sure I'd do that just yet," Banjo counseled. "I heard the ground covering the grave was cut with a sod cutter. Not a lot of people have access to something like that."

"I'm pretty sure you can rent them. And if someone did rent one there would be a record of it. I think I'll check into that."

"The killer could have rented the device on the mainland and then brought it over on the ferry," Banjo pointed out.

"That's true. Maybe the possession of a sod cutter won't turn out to be a clue at all. It's frustrating when you think you're on to something and then realize you really aren't."

"Victory comes to those with the patience to wait," Banjo reminded me.

"Yeah, well, we both know I'm not the patient type. Did you know Roxi?" I asked.

"Not well, but she did stop in here from time to time and we'd chat. Summer didn't care for her; she was pretty aggressive in her bid for attention from the male members of the community."

I picked up a piece of driftwood that had been carved to resemble a pelican. It was really very good. I could see why Banjo's creations were so popular with the tourists.

"I heard she'd been going out a lot since Jimmy passed," I commented. "She must just have been lonely."

"I saw her on the beach a week or two ago. She was with a guy, and she certainly didn't look lonely, if you know what I mean."

"When was that exactly?" I wondered.

Banjo appeared to be thinking about it. "It must have been the week before she turned up missing. It was late, probably around ten. There was a full moon and I decided to take a walk because Summer had turned in early with a headache. I happened across the couple, who were halfway to happyland, if you get my meaning. The only reason I knew it was Roxi for sure was because her red hair coupled with that Texas drawl made her pretty distinctive."

"And the guy? Do you know who it was?"

"No. Didn't see his face. But he had dark hair and a dark tan that showed off his white backside."

"Do you think either Roxi or her date saw you?"

"I'm sure they didn't. They were pretty distracted."

"Yeah, I bet. I should get going. I still have one more delivery to make and it looks like it's going to start raining any minute."

Banjo looked out the window toward the darkening sky on the horizon.

"You have a couple of hours. Maybe more. I've spent a lot of years on the water and I can usually call things pretty close. I'd say these clouds are just the preshow."

"I hope so. I'd like to get home before the worst of it hits."

After I left Ship Wreck I continued down the street to the Bait and Stitch. One of the last places Roxi had been seen was at the Thursday night meeting of the Mystery Lovers Book Club. The club was planning to move to Coffee Cat Books in October, but for now it continued to gather in the sewing room of the Bait and Stitch, as it had for years. It occurred to me it was possible one of the members of the book club might know something that could help identify her killer.

"Afternoon," I called. "I have your books." I handed the package to Marley, who was sitting with Maggie and four other women at the quilting table, although none of them were quilting.

"Oh, good, I've been anxious to start that new mystery series I ordered," Marley said after accepting the package and taking a peek inside.

"Tara ordered some extra copies for inventory because you recommended the author so highly," I informed Marley.

"I'm sure they'll sell. The author is really good, and she writes several different series."

"We were just talking about our costumes for the ball on Saturday," Maggie shared. "I'm trying to decide between my Marie Antoinette costume and my Scarlett O'Hara."

"I'm sure either will create quite a stir," I assured her.

Both gowns were low cut and Aunt Maggie had been blessed with an ample bosom.

"Who are you going to dress as?" I asked Marley.

"I thought I'd wear my Queen Victoria costume. Your aunt is trying to talk me into something a little more daring, but I think I'll leave daring to her. How about you, dear? What do you plan to wear?"

"I really have no idea," I answered honestly.

"The ball is next weekend," Marley reminded me.

"I know. I guess I'll figure something out."

"So tell us," Lillian Vale, one of the quilters, asked, "are you going to look into Roxi's murder? Cody's story caused quite a stir. I spoke to him earlier, and he told me that he not only sold out of the first run of the weekend edition of the paper but the second run as well. I guess he's pretty stoked about all the new advertisers he's managed to line up for the next couple of weeks."

"It seems odd to be happy about someone's success when it's the result of the murder of one of our own," Marley commented. "Still, I *am* happy Cody is doing well. I was tickled pink when I found out he was going to start up the paper. Things just weren't the same without it."

"So are you planning to investigate?" Maggie asked.

"I'm not sure," I answered. "Tara and I are pretty busy with the bookstore, but Cody did ask us to help him brainstorm about possible leads. He really wants to have something new to report in the midweek edition of the paper."

"I'm afraid you're going to find all kinds of leads when it comes to identifying who might have wanted Roxi dead," Doris Rutherford, the queen bee of the local gossip circuit, commented.

"I've heard from a few people that she'd been going out a lot since Jimmy died," I responded.

"Rolanda Perkins told me that she saw Roxi hanging all over Tony Sommers a few nights before she was murdered," Doris continued. "And with Tony's wife about to have a baby and all. I felt bad that Roxi lost Jimmy, but she had no right to go snooping around men who were already taken."

I knew Tony had dark hair and a dark tan, but so did more than half the men on the island.

"Roxi might have been fooling around with Tony, but I heard she was thinking about shacking up with Greg Westlake," quilting circle member and book club enthusiast Olivia Oxford informed me.

Greg Westlake? Greg was kind of a nerd. He didn't seem to be Roxi's type at all.

"How do you know?" I asked.

"Greg's mama told me. She said Greg had already informed her that he was moving out of her basement and in with Roxi. I have to say Greg's mama was none too happy about that. Greg is a good boy. The last thing a mama wants is for her little boy to end up with a woman like Roxi."

Little boy? Greg was a thirty-five-year-old pizza delivery man. I would think his mother would be happy to see him end up with *anyone*.

"At least Greg was single," I commented.

"Single or not, his mama was about as mad as I've ever seen her. If you ask me, I think the woman had a girl in mind for her son once he finished sowing his wild oats."

"Greg doesn't seem like the type who would let his mama pick out his wife," I commented.

"I wouldn't be too sure," Olivia argued. "Greg's mama has a lot more influence over him and his decisions than you might think. Besides, have you seen her? She's built like a linebacker and Greg is such a puny kid. My guess is that he's scared to death of her."

"I heard Greg was offered a chance to go to South America with that friend of his from the pizza place, but his mom put the kibosh on the whole idea," Doris added.

"Seems like he's old enough to make his own decisions," Maggie commented.

"Maybe, but I don't blame his mama," Doris insisted. "That kid he works with is bad news."

I listened as the group began to discuss other members of the community who were *bad news*. In most cases the conservative senior women who took part in the conversation were being just that: conservative. Still, Doris did have a point about the kid from the pizza joint. The guy had always given me the creeps. If I found out tomorrow that he was a serial killer I wouldn't be the least bit surprised.

"Were you at the book club on the Thursday before Roxi died?" I asked Maggie, who had remained uncharacteristically quiet during the exchange.

"I was."

"And how did she seem?"

Maggie shrugged. "She seemed like Roxi. She really enjoyed her mysteries and she always had a lot to share. That night was no different. She seemed cheerful and happy to be there. If something was going on that led to her death she didn't let on."

"Did she mention any plans she might have had for the weekend?" I wondered.

"Not that I remember."

"She did say something about meeting someone on Saturday," Marley reminded Maggie.

"You're right. I think it was someone she knew from work," Maggie informed me, "but I can't be sure."

"You might talk to Molly," Marley suggested. Molly was the cashier at the Driftwood Café. "It seems the two of them had been tight of late."

I spoke to the women for a few more minutes and then moved on to the Driftwood to see if Molly was on shift. She wasn't, but the person who was covering the cash register confirmed that both Roxi and Molly were off over the past weekend, so it was possible they'd planned to get together to do something. Molly wasn't due to come in again until the following Monday, so I thanked the woman I spoke to and headed back to the bookstore.

I looked up into the sky. It wasn't looking good. I hoped Banjo's weather-predicting abilities were as accurate as he'd assured me.

Chapter 3

Kayla and Karla were waiting for me when I arrived at the oceanfront estate where I lived. Maggie lives in the main house, which is huge, while I live in the summer cabin, which is tiny. Also on the property is Harthaven Cat Sanctuary, which Maggie founded to protect the island's feral cat population after Mayor Bradley made it legal to remove cats from your property using any means at your disposal.

Sugar and Spice were sisters who had come to us at a very young age. Sugar was pure white, while Spice was sort of a cinnamon color. Both kittens had round faces and long hair, and both were totally adorable.

"So who gets which kitten?" I asked.

"Spice will be mine," Karla informed me. "Although I don't suppose it will matter because we'll all be living in the same small apartment."

"I'm sure you'll enjoy the girls. They're box trained and very affectionate. They've had their shots and have been spayed, so you should be good on that front for a year. Are you all set up with kitten food and litter boxes?"

"We're ready. We bought everything we'd need right after you confirmed that we could have them this morning," Kayla informed me.

"We're really very excited," Karla joined in.

"I'm glad your new landlord is cool with kitties. I'm sure Sugar and Spice will make awesome pets. You do live on a busy street, though, so be sure to keep them inside. We wouldn't want them to get hit by a car."

"We will," both girls assured me.

After I saw Karla, Kayla, and their new pets off, I cleaned litter boxes and then provided all our residents with food and water. It was a lot of work caring for the cats, which needed to be tended to twice each day. Maggie and I generally shared the work generated by the cat sanctuary, but even with the two of us, the chores seemed never-ending. We'd talked about hiring part-time help now that Haley, our summertime helper, had returned home, but so far neither of us had gotten around to searching for the right person.

Once I'd completed my chores, I grabbed my dog Max and headed down the beach for a very quick run. It appeared Banjo had been correct in his forecast. The sky was dark and heavy with clouds, and the meteorologists were still calling for rain, but so far we hadn't had a single drop. I knew I'd need to make the run fast, but Max needed the exercise after being cooped up in the cabin all day. I, on the other hand, didn't have an overabundance of excess energy after my long day at the bookstore, so I just walked along the shoreline as Max ran down the beach, chasing the seagulls and bald eagles that had come out to find their evening meals in the low tide.

During the summer it was easy to make time to spend outdoors, but as the days grew shorter I knew it would be harder to squeeze in walks on the beach as I tried to manage the other obligations of my life. I hated to leave Max alone for so much of the day. I'd thought I might bring him to work and let him hang out in the cat lounge, but I was afraid his presence would distract from the cats we were trying to place. Maybe I'd see if the *Madrona Island News* needed a doggy mascot on the days I worked.

As I walked, I could hear thunder rolling in from the distance. It sounded like the storm was finally going to make its way ashore. I turned around and headed back toward my cabin. I found I was looking forward to spending the evening with my brother and my two best friends, even if the main topic of conversation would be the death of a neighbor.

By the time I returned to the cabin it was starting to sprinkle. I made a fire and then headed up to my bedroom for dry clothes before the others arrived.

I fed Max and then opened a couple of bottles of wine. I wasn't sure what Cody planned to bring over for dinner, but I hoped he'd hurry up and get here. I was starving.

"It's really starting to come down out there," Danny, who was the first to arrive, commented as he came in through the side door. "I hope it lets up before tomorrow. I have four tours going out."

"I heard the storm is supposed to blow through by morning, so you should be fine. How did things go today?" I asked as he helped himself to a beer from my refrigerator.

"It was a good day. I've been pretty lucky with the weather so far this season, but I can feel change in the air."

"If you have four tours tomorrow I take it you won't be at church or at Mom's for dinner."

"Sorry. I need to make my money while I can."

"Mom isn't going to be happy that you missed three Sundays in a row."

"Mom is going to have to learn that I'm an adult and going home to Sunday dinner isn't always going to be a priority."

I understood what Danny was saying. I'd had similar thoughts on other occasions, but so far I hadn't had the courage to defy my mom and actually turn my back on tradition. Ever since I was born, Sundays had been reserved for attending Mass at St. Patrick's Catholic Church, followed by supper at my mom's house. When Tara and I opened Coffee Cat Books we'd discussed being open on Sundays, but in the end we'd decided that our obligation to church and family was more important than the additional profit being open might bring us.

"Have you heard from Aiden?" I asked about my oldest brother, who had been in Alaska following the fish since June.

"Not in a few weeks, but the last time I spoke to him, he thought he'd be home the first part of October. I imagine that, like me, he's trying to squeeze what he can out of the nice weather we've been having. It'll be good to have him back.

Maybe he can deflect some of Mom's mothering."

"Each time he returns I think that maybe he'll settle down and stay, but then, come summer, he's off again, chasing the fish."

"Fishing is in his blood." Danny took a swig of his beer, than sat down on one of the bar stools that lined the counter separating the kitchen from the living room.

"I guess. At least he's home most of the year, unlike Siobhan, who never comes home at all."

"Siobhan is just trying to live her own life."

Danny was right. I guess I understood how Siobhan, who didn't really get along all that well with our mother, would prefer to stay in Seattle, where she probably wasn't treated like a child. Still, I missed my older sister and wished she'd make the trip to the island a little more often.

I watched as Tara pulled up in her car and dashed into the cabin with her kitten, Bandit, under her sweatshirt. She set him on the floor and he immediately pounced on Max.

I laughed as Max barked once in greeting and then sank into downward-dog position to greet the rambunctious kitten.

Tara pulled off her wet sweatshirt and hung it near the fire to dry. "I heard there are flash-flood warnings out for low-lying areas," she informed us. "I think the storm is supposed to blow through quickly but dump quite a bit of rain on its way. Maybe up to several inches."

"I guess we could use the water, but I do hope there isn't any serious flooding. Last time there was a flood the peninsula road was inaccessible for almost two days."

"I'm sure things will be fine." Tara looked around the room. "Cody's not here? I'm starving."

"He texted to say he'd be a few minutes late, but he should be here soon. I have cheese and crackers to go with the wine if you want something to tide you over."

"I guess I'll wait a few minutes," Tara answered as she poured herself a glass of wine. "I'd hate to get filled up on crackers only to find he brought something from Antonio's. I've been craving Italian all day."

"I do remember him saying something about Antonio's," I confirmed.

"By the way," Tara turned to Danny, "did you get my message about the group who wanted to change their reservation from tomorrow to next Sunday?"

Tara and I had taken over the reservation system for Danny after we opened the bookstore. Between the two of us, we'd mostly handled the reservations for *Hart of the Sea* anyway, but now that we had the shop on the wharf we had an actual reservation counter.

Danny frowned and pulled his phone out of his pocket. "Sorry, I didn't check my messages when I came in from my last tour."

"You really need to stay on top of things," Tara scolded. "If I hadn't seen you this evening you would have prepared for an eight a.m. tour for nothing."

"I guess that would have been my problem," Danny shot back.

I hated to see Danny and Tara bicker, and it seemed they'd been doing a lot more of it lately. I suppose the added tension could be due to the fact that uberorganized Tara was handling the scheduling for over-the-top disorganized Danny on a daily rather than occasional basis. The two really were at opposite ends of the spectrum. But in spite of this obvious conclusion, I was pretty sure the tension had more to do with the unresolved feelings they were fighting since the sleep kiss they'd shared a couple of months before.

"It looks like there are headlights on the peninsula road," I informed them in an attempt to change the subject and dispel the tension. "I hope that's Cody with our dinner."

Thankfully, I was right and the car did belong to Cody, who pulled into the drive and then turned left, away from the main house and toward my cabin on the beach. He got out and ran toward the deck, and I noticed he didn't have any food in his hands, which made me a little nervous.

"Look what I found sitting in the rocking chair outside," Cody said as he walked in through my side door. He held a beautiful calico cat in his arms.

"Must be Beatrice," I commented.

"Beatrice?"

"I'll explain later. Did you bring food?"

"I did. Why don't you take the cat and I'll get the food?"

Cody must have read Tara's mind because he had ordered food from Antonio's. He brought two lasagnas, one sausage with marinara and one seafood with alfredo. He also brought garlic bread and salad with Antonio's special dressing.

I took a few minutes to get Beatrice settled in. I showed her where the cat box was and then prepared fresh bowls of food and water. She ate some food, used the box, and settled down on the sofa in front of the fire for a nap. Then I returned to the kitchen, my friends, and dinner.

"So how did your investigation go?" I asked Cody after we had all served ourselves.

"I'm not sure. On one hand, I've been given a list of potential leads by a variety of people. On the other, none of them seems likely to end up anywhere. Still, I suppose it wouldn't hurt to follow up."

"What leads?" I asked.

Cody took a sip of wine before he continued. The poor guy looked exhausted. He'd been working long hours since he'd reopened the paper.

"I spoke to Ernie Wall, Roxi's boss at the Driftwood Café. He said Roxi was a hard worker who was well liked by her customers but that something had been going on lately. She was a real mess after Jimmy died, so he gave her a month off with pay. When she returned she seemed to be back to her old self for a few weeks, and then about six weeks ago she started coming in late and even missing her shift on a couple of occasions. Ernie asked her about it and she told him that she was having some financial issues so she'd taken another job, tending bar at O'Malley's in the evenings. Ernie said he tried to help her out with some money, but he didn't think it was enough."

"If she was up half the night tending bar I guess that would explain her tendency to sleep in," I offered.

"It would, but the thing is that I spoke to O'Malley too, and he said that while she did hang out in the bar most evenings, she wasn't working for him."

"The fact that she'd been hanging out in the bar fits with what I've learned as well," I confirmed. "It sounds like she'd been marathon dating since Jimmy passed."

"I'd seen her in the bar almost every time I'd been in," Danny confirmed, "and on each of those occasions she was with a different guy. Jimmy was my friend and I cared about Roxi, so I hate to say anything that might cast a bad light on her, but it seems like she might have been dating for money."

"She was working as a hooker?" Tara asked.

"It's just a hunch. An unsubstantiated hunch, so I'd recommend we be careful about who we mention it to," Danny answered.

"Do you have any reason to believe Roxi was in trouble financially?" Tara asked Danny.

"I don't see how she wouldn't be," Danny reasoned. "Jimmy made more money than she did, and now his income is gone, and it ain't cheap to bury someone these days."

"Which brings me to my next lead," Cody offered. "I went down to the harbor to talk to the people who have boats docked near Jimmy's, and the woman who lives in the first slip in her row told me Roxi met a man at the boat on several occasions."

"Did you happen to ask when she saw this man?" I wondered.

"I did, but she claimed she couldn't really remember. She did say that while Roxi refused to discuss who he was or why they'd met, she seemed to be afraid of him."

"Are you thinking the guy might have been some sort of money lender or maybe an employee of a money lender?" I asked.

I took a second helping of seafood lasagna while Cody gathered his thoughts before continuing. This had to be the best seafood lasagna I'd ever eaten. The lobster was plentiful, the scallops cooked to perfection, the crab fresh, and the shrimp tender. Once you added the thick white sauce, homemade pasta, and melted cheese, it was a meal to die for.

"It's a theory," Cody confirmed.

"So we suspect Roxi was in financial trouble, we know she'd been dating a lot of men lately, and we think she might have been using those dates to raise funds," Tara summarized. "Did you learn anything else?"

"I picked up another lead at the church," Cody answered.

"The church?" I asked. "That doesn't seem to fit with the rest of the story."

"I agree, which was why I found it so interesting." Cody sat back in his chair. "I knew Roxi had last been seen at her book club meeting, so I decided to see if I could track down a few members to see if they had any insight as to what Roxi's plans for last weekend were. I spoke to a woman named Angie who's both a book club member and a library volunteer. Angie told me Roxi also was active at the Tuesday night children's program held at St. Patrick's. It seems she'd been volunteering there since right after Jimmy died."

I frowned. "It's odd that we didn't know that. You and I are at the church every Wednesday night for choir practice and Tara is there all the time helping Sister Mary out with the children's programs."

"I really haven't been around there as often as I used to be," Tara countered. "I still help out, but once we began working on the bookstore I cut way back. I'm really only there on Sundays most weeks now."

"Yeah, and you and I are only at the church on Wednesdays and Sundays," Cody added to me.

"I guess that's true. So what did you learn?"

"Sister Mary was away today, so I wasn't able to speak to her. I plan to go back there tomorrow. Angie seemed to think Roxi did a good job with the group and that the kids really liked her."

"It does sound like we have an intriguing mystery on our hands. I can't wait to see how it all works out. Does anyone want any more wine?" I asked.

"I'll have some." Danny held up his glass. "I think the weather's getting worse." The sound of the rain slamming into the front of the cabin had intensified since we'd been talking. "Maybe I'll stay here tonight instead of going back to the boat."

"My couch is your couch," I offered.

"I was thinking of risking the rain and going up to Maggie's. She has actual beds."

"Suit yourself." I shrugged.

Danny often stayed at Maggie's when the weather was bad; trying to sleep on a boat that was being rocked by a storm was no fun at all.

"Bandit and I might take you up on your sofa if it doesn't let up before it's time to go," Tara said. "It's really coming down hard."

"You're welcome to stay."

Tara picked up her kitten and snuggled him to her chest.

"Cody?" I asked, as long as I was asking everyone else.

"I live next door. I think I can make it." He laughed.

"Maybe, but you'll most likely get soaked clear through."

"I've been soaked by rain before."

"Yeah, I guess we all have," I agreed.

"Remember that summer we hiked up to that old deserted lookout tower on the far side of the island and it started raining?" Tara reminded us. "Aiden and his girl of the moment and Siobhan and her guy were with us as well. I'm not sure why we didn't just stay there and wait out the storm, but I do remember we were all wet and muddy by the time we got home."

"We *were* going to stay in the tower and wait it out, but it started to lightning and Aiden's girl totally freaked out," Cody said.

"That's right. She went running out into the storm and Aiden followed her."

"And when we realized Aiden wasn't coming back we all went after them," I said.

"The girl was totally freaked," Cody added. "She ran so fast she wasn't looking where she was going and she slipped and fell down the hill and sprained her ankle. Aiden, Danny, and I had to take turns carrying her back down the mountain. It was pouring rain and muddy as heck, with lightning crashing all around us, but the thing I remember most about that trip down the hill was that the girl was so hysterical every time thunder came crashing down around us that she dug her talonlike fake nails into my back. I'm pretty sure I still have the scars."

"I remember that now. What was her name?" I asked.

"Sheila," Danny said.

"No, I think it was Sherry," Cody countered.

"Shelly," Tara said with conviction.

"Yeah, I think Tara's right; it was Shelly. Those were good times."

"The best," everyone agreed.

I sat back in my chair and smiled as Beatrice got up from her nap and came over to join me. There are many wonderful things in life, but there's nothing better than sharing a meal with good friends who also share your history.

Chapter 4

Sunday, September 20

I woke up the next morning to sunshine. It looked like Tara was correct; the storm had blown through during the night. I knew I should get up and get started on my day, but the warmth of Max curled up on my left and Beatrice on my right was something I wanted to take a minute to savor. After the rain the previous night I could smell a new freshness in the air. I like to sleep with my window open on all but the coldest nights. The sound of the waves crashing outside my little cabin always made me feel linked to the natural wonder that existed around me. The steady rhythm of the tide almost lulled me back to sleep, but I knew I had things to attend to before I left for Harthaven for the day, so I forced myself to toss back the covers, pull on a sweatshirt, and head downstairs.

There was a note from Tara telling me that she'd gone home to shower and change before Mass. I still had a couple of hours before I had to leave, so I let Max out, fed both animals, and then headed upstairs to dress. My mom wasn't a big fan of animals in her house, and of course they weren't allowed inside the church, so once again I'd be forced to leave poor Max alone.

I quickly pulled on thick sweats and a knit cap and headed out the door with Max on my heels. If I hurried, he and I could go for a run and I'd still have time to shower and dress before I had to leave for the day.

"I've been thinking about speaking to Cody about letting you hang out with him at the paper during the day when I'm at the bookstore. Would you like that?"

Max barked once before he took off, chasing a colony of seagulls that had landed on the beach. The smell of salt tickled my senses as I took a deep breath of the fresh morning air. Although it was chilly so early in the morning, the sun was bright and the sky clear. It looked like it was going to be a perfect fall day.

"I know it's been tough since the bookstore opened and I've been gone so much," I continued after Max had sent the birds into the air and returned to my side. "I think we're going to need to adjust our schedules a bit so that you aren't alone so much. I'm sure you could go over to stay with Mr. Parsons and Rambler when Cody can't take you."

Max appeared to be indifferent to my comments, but I was certain he really did care deeply about the outcome of this conversation. I'd been home at least part of most days before the bookstore opened and now I was away more often than not between work, church, family, and community obligations.

I stopped running when I saw a whale breach in the distance. No matter how often I witness the presence of whales in the area I still find myself in awe every time I happen across one. There was a boat nearby that looked like it could be Danny, but I knew his first tour had canceled. Danny was the only whale watch tour still operating this late in the year, so I had to assume the boat I saw was privately owned.

"Big boat. I wonder who it belongs to," I said aloud.

Max didn't know, so I shrugged and continued on my way. It wasn't unusual to have visitors to the island who owned yachts larger than most islanders' homes.

"So what do you think of Beatrice?" I asked Max, who didn't answer. "She's really beautiful and so affectionate. I'm kind of sorry to say this, but I have a feeling she won't be with us for long. The others only stayed until the mystery they were sent to solve was done."

Max ran into the surf to grab a stick that was floating on the surface.

"I keep waiting for her to do something."

Max dropped the stick at my feet, which I had to avoid stepping on as I jogged along.

"She only just arrived last night. I guess I should give her time to settle in."

I looked at Max, who had returned to the water to fetch something else. I should have paused as I watched him swim out to the large object that was just a bit farther out than I was really comfortable with, but instead I kept running only to trip over a log that had washed up in the storm and fall hard on my left shoulder.

It knocked the wind out of me for a minute. Max ran back to me as soon as he saw me fall and was frantically licking my face while I struggled to catch my breath.

"Max, off," I managed to say.

Max whined but obeyed. He sat down next to me and waited for me to get up.

I rolled over onto my back and carefully moved my limbs. Nothing appeared to be broken, but I had a huge gash on my shoulder where I'd landed on a piece of the log.

I took several deep breaths as I fought momentary dizziness.

"Are you okay?"

I looked up. It was Cody.

"What are you doing here?" I asked.

"I was down the beach walking Rambler. I saw you fall. I ran as quickly as I could, but I was pretty far away."

Cody knelt down on the sand next to me. "Did you hit your head?"

"No. Just my shoulder."

Cody took off his sweatshirt and wrapped it around my arm, which had begun to bleed. "Can you stand?"

I offered Cody a hand and he helped me to my feet.

"I'm fine. I just had the wind knocked out of me."

"Your shoulder looks pretty bad. We need to get it cleaned up. Do you have any antiseptic?"

"I have something even better," I said as I remembered the salve Tansy had sent.

Cody helped me back to the cabin and I took a hot shower while he made coffee. I tried to get him to go on home and change out of his damp clothing, but he insisted he wanted to stay long enough to help me dress my wound. It felt nice to have someone fuss over me, although I would have preferred to be less of a klutz.

"See, I'm fine," I said after I'd cleaned myself up and changed into dry and sand-free clothing.

"What happened, anyway? One minute you were jogging in my direction and the next you where facedown in the sand."

"I was watching Max swim out after something in the water and not looking where I was going. That log wasn't there yesterday. I guess it washed up in the storm last night. I should have been paying more attention."

Cody took my forearm in his and looked more closely at the angry red wound on my shoulder.

"You said you have something to put on it?" he asked.

"Tansy sent this. It appears she predicted I was going to be a klutz. I have some bandages. I'm sure I'll be fine."

Cody rubbed some of Tansy's salve into my shoulder and covered it with a large bandage.

"I need to go home to change for church, but I'll be back by to get you."

"I can drive myself."

"I know you can, but we're going to the same place so I may as well drive you. I'll be back in an hour."

"I'm going to Mom's after church," I reminded him.

"I know. She invited me to dinner as well. Now eat the eggs and toast I made for you and take it easy until I get back. You fell pretty hard. You could still have a reaction."

"Yes, Dad."

I watched as Cody left and then started in on the eggs he'd made while I was in the shower. They were scrambled and baked in the oven with cheese and mushrooms. They really were delicious. Maybe I should let him come to my rescue more often.

"Sorry, the eggs have cheese, which isn't good for cats," I said to Beatrice, who had jumped up onto the chair next to me and was watching each forkful as it traveled from my plate to my mouth. "I have salmon treats in the cupboard that I'll be happy to dig out after I finish eating."

The cat meowed and jumped off the chair. She trotted into the living room and curled up on the sofa while I finished my meal. The fact that Beatrice hadn't actually done anything yet almost made me wonder if she *was* Beatrice. Based on the timing of her arrival, I'd assumed she was, but the other cats Tansy had sent would have been leading me across town or knocking stuff off shelves by now. Beatrice seemed content to nap.

By the time Cody and I arrived at the church most of the kids were waiting in the choir room. Luckily, Tara had arrived early and had done a good job of getting everyone ready to go on.

"What happened to your shoulder?" she asked when she noticed the large bandage.

"Tripped while jogging. Tansy sent a salve, so I'm sure it'll be fine. Have you seen Trina?"

Trina McDonald was supposed to do a solo that day, but I didn't see her in the crowd.

"She was nervous, so Sister Mary asked her to help hand out flyers for the Harvest Festival. She's ready to go on, but the waiting was killing her, so Sister Mary decided a diversion was in order."

"That was probably a good move."

I looked around the room. The children's choir currently featured twenty-three boys and girls between the ages of five and twelve. When I'd first been asked to colead the group I wasn't sure I wanted to take on this level of commitment, but it turned out I was having the best time with Cody and the kids.

"I don't see either of the Paulson girls," I added, mentioning sisters Serenity and Trinity.

"One of the other girls said something about Destiny and her mom fighting again," Tara informed me.

Destiny is the oldest Paulson offspring at sixteen.

"It seems like the whole family has been in crisis ever since Destiny found out she was pregnant," Tara continued. "I know her mom is really trying to deal with things the best she can, but she's a single mom herself, with two jobs and three kids. I just don't think she has the energy to deal with Destiny's mood swings."

"Maybe I'll talk to her," I offered.

"Mrs. Paulson?"

"Actually, I was referring to Destiny, but yeah, maybe I'll try talking to both of them. Not that I'm an expert on pregnant teenagers, but I hate to see such a nice family fall apart."

"It seems Destiny has been worse since the baby's father left the island," Tara offered. "I'm sure she's terrified of what the future might bring and is acting out as a way of dealing with emotions she doesn't have an outlet for, but I heard her mom is at the end of her rope. I even heard she might send her away."

"Really? Is it that bad?"

"I think it's become that bad, and I'm sure Mrs. Paulson is concerned about how this whole thing is affecting the younger two."

"I don't blame her. It does seem that Destiny has been lashing out at everyone she comes into contact with. It can't be easy to live with someone who's intent on making everyone as miserable as she is."

"Ms. Caitlin—" Sasha Walton, an adorable little girl with dark skin, huge dark eyes, and curly black hair, interrupted our conversation.

"Yes, Sasha. What can I do for you?"

"Tommy has a frog in his pocket. A big one. He wants to sneak it into Mass and then let it go when no one is looking."

"Great." I sighed. I looked around the room to find Tommy whispering to his friend Jett in the corner of the room. It looked like they were in on the prank together.

"Why don't you go help Cody get the kids lined up and I'll deal with Tommy?" I suggested to Tara. "We can talk about this more after Mass. You're coming to dinner?"

"I wouldn't miss it."

I took Sasha's hand and walked her across the room to where the boys were giggling as they looked at something one of them was holding.

"Nice frog," I commented as I walked up behind them. "He have a name?"

"We just call him Toad," Tommy informed me.

"Well, he's a right handsome frog, but I'm afraid Toad will have to wait here in the choir room until after Mass. Do you have a box for him?"

"No," Tommy admitted.

"Then how about we either find a box or let him go outside near Father Kilian's koi pond?"

Tommy looked at Jett, who shrugged.

"I'm guessing we'll let him go," Tommy decided.

"Cody is lining everyone up. Why don't you go get in line and I'll take Toad out to the pond?" I offered.

Tommy handed me the small reptile.

"I'll meet everyone inside once I introduce Toad to his new home," I informed the group.

I let myself out through the back door of the building. Father Kilian has the most beautiful flower garden on the island. Even though it was beginning to die off as the days grew shorter, there was still plenty of fall color to create a peaceful and appealing setting.

I gently placed Toad onto the muddy surface at the edge of the pond. He hopped under a large fern and waited for me to leave. I knew I needed to get back inside, but it was so serene and peaceful out here alone in the garden.

I caught a movement out of the corner of my eye as I turned to leave. I couldn't be certain, but it looked like it might have been Destiny watching from the other side of the property. I thought about going after her but hesitated. I really should get inside, and I wasn't 100 percent certain it was her anyway.

I felt so bad for the poor girl. She seemed intent on pushing away everyone in her life, but I knew she must be terrified about what her future might hold. I wasn't even certain what she planned to do about the baby when it was born, but adoption seemed to be the logical choice. Destiny couldn't raise the baby on her own, and the last thing her mother needed was another mouth to feed. I considered how difficult it must be to come to the decision to let your baby go. To be honest,

I wasn't sure what I would do in her situation.

I glanced one final time in the direction in which I had seen the movement, but whomever had been there was gone. I could hear the organ just beginning to play the opening hymn inside the church. I said a quick prayer for Destiny and her family and hurried back inside.

Chapter 5

Sunday dinner at the Hart family home was a tradition that had been around since before I was born. I'll admit that in recent years there have been those Sundays when the only people in attendance were my younger sister Cassidy, Mom, and me, but this week Aunt Maggie, Marley, Tara, and Cody had joined us.

Still, even with the extra guests, dinner at the Hart house was nothing like the huge gatherings we'd had back before the cannery closed and most of my aunts and uncles moved away. Our gatherings shrank even further when Dad died and Siobhan moved to Seattle.

I walked into the kitchen to find the others working together to prepare the communal meal. Mom grabbed Cody before he even got through the door and instructed him to set up the patio table outdoors. It had turned out to be a beautiful afternoon and she wanted to enjoy her flower garden for as long as she could before winter set in.

"Caitlin, why don't you make a salad?" Mom instructed.

I'm not sure if the fact that I'm *always* asked to make the salad is an indication of my mother's lack of faith in my cooking ability or if it's because I'm usually the last one to stagger in and the salad is the only job that hasn't been assigned yet.

"We were just discussing the Harvest Festival next weekend," Tara, who was stirring something on the stove, caught me up. "They're going to open the corn maze and hay rides on Thursday rather than Friday this year."

"It does seem like the event would do better if there were more options to attend," I agreed. "Are we planning to have a booth over the weekend?"

"I'd like to," Tara responded, "but I hate to close the store on Friday and Saturday."

"I can handle the booth in town if you can find someone to help at the store," I offered.

"Cassidy is off school beginning on Friday," Mom informed us. "I'm sure she'd be happy to help."

"Great; I'll ask her," Tara answered.

"Speaking of help," Mom continued, "I've been elected chairperson for the Friday night supper at the church and I could really use everyone's help. Our women's group hopes to earn enough money to buy new linens for the sanctuary this year."

"I can help," I confirmed.

"Excellent." Mom opened the oven door and took a peek at whatever was inside. It certainly did smell good.

"We've decided to set up a kiddie carnival in the Sunday school rooms. I was hoping you and Tara could help with that. Maggie and Marley have volunteered to help me in the kitchen."

I shrugged. "Whatever you need."

"I really think this is going to be our most profitable festival ever," Mom exclaimed.

"I heard the tickets to the Masquerade Ball are selling like hot cakes," Marley commented.

"I think everyone is hoping for a repeat of last year's entertainment," Maggie snickered.

Last year one of the local women dumped an entire pitcher of punch over her husband's head when she saw he was flirting with one of the waitresses from O'Malley's. He'd tried to chase after her, but he slipped and fell, which set off a series of events rivaling the best slapstick comedy ever featured on the silver screen. The majority of the attendees felt both husband and wife had acted inappropriately, but I thought the whole thing was a hoot.

"Of course this year all anyone will be talking about is Madrona Island's most recent murder," Marley speculated.

"It does seem to be at the forefront of most conversations," Mom agreed. "I haven't heard anything about an arrest as of yet."

"As far as I know, Finn isn't even close to getting it figured out," I said. Ryan Finnegan is the resident deputy who's officially investigating the case. "He's been chasing down some leads, but as of yesterday he'd come up empty. I didn't see him at Mass this morning, so I imagine he's working. Maybe he'll get things wrapped up by tomorrow."

"The whole thing is just so disturbing." Mom sighed. "I just ran into Roxi at the church a couple of weeks ago and it seemed like she was finally beginning to deal with Jimmy's death. I can't imagine what could have happened or who would have wanted to kill her."

"Roxi might have appeared as though she was dealing with things better, but based on what I've heard the past couple of days, I don't think she was at all," I commented.

"I spoke to Sister Mary about her," Tara spoke up. "She confirmed that Roxi had been active in her Tuesday night group and that she really was wonderful with the kids. Sister Mary has heard the rumors about Roxi's recent behavior, but in her opinion there may be more to what's going on than people think. She said Roxi seemed lost. She tried to talk to her about whatever problems she'd been having, but Roxi was evasive. Still, she said she'd been around her enough to think she was a good person who simply had a huge problem she didn't know how to deal with. Sister Mary feels we shouldn't go with the easy answer, that we should dig deeper. I don't know about you, but I trust her judgment."

I nodded. "Yeah. Me too."

"Cait, can you grab the linen napkins out of the hutch?" Mom asked.

I left the kitchen and entered the dining room where the hutch was located. As I passed, my sister grabbed my arm and pulled me into the hallway.

"I need your help," she whispered.

"What kind of help?"

Cassie pulled me into the den and closed the door behind us.

"I have a date, so I need to get out of here early."

"Did you tell Mom about your date?" I wondered.

"No. She doesn't approve of Brad; she'd never let me go."

"Brad?" I asked as I sat down on the same sofa I used to lounge on when I was a child. "I thought you were dating a guy named Justin."

Cassie rolled her eyes. "Where have you been? Justin was over months ago."

I was glad to hear that because Justin was almost three years older than sixteen-year-old Cassie.

"Have I met Brad?"

"Not yet. We've been keeping it casual, but I really like him. I know I should have told him I couldn't go out with him tonight, but I found myself saying I'd love to have an early dinner with him. He's really cute," Cassie added, as if that explained everything.

"And this Brad—does he go to school with you?"

Cassie nodded. "He's a junior like me and yes, he's a nice guy."

I'd heard that before. I'm afraid Cassie tended to gravitate toward bad boys.

"So why doesn't Mom like him?"

"I don't know," Cassie insisted. "He's great."

I just looked at her.

"He does have a unique style."

I continued to wait.

"It's his hair," Cassie finally admitted.

"What's wrong with his hair?"

"It's blue."

I frowned. "I'm sure Mom wouldn't be thrilled with blue hair, but I don't see her forbidding you to date this boy based on hair color alone."

"She doesn't like his tats."

"He has a tattoo?"

"Several of them, actually. But they really work with his piercings."

No wonder Mom didn't want Cassie getting in a car alone with this boy. Mom was very conservative. I'd had to wait to get my ears pierced until I was eighteen.

"Look, I know how it sounds, but Brad is nice. Really. You have to provide a diversion so I can sneak out."

I leaned back against the sofa cushion behind me and let out a long breath. I really hate these moments when I'm torn between my roles as supportive big sister and responsible adult. I really did understand where Cassie was coming from. Sort of. I'd snuck out during my tenure as a teenager in this house and on several of those occasions Siobhan had covered for me. On the other hand, I didn't know this new boyfriend of Cassie's.

For all I knew, my mom had a really good reason for not wanting her to go out with him.

"I know how important it is to have freedom when you're sixteen," I began, "but it's Sunday. Sundays are important to Mom. Why don't you call Brad and invite him to join us for dinner?"

"Haven't you been listening? Mom hates him."

"I'm sure she doesn't *hate* him."

"She does."

"How about if I talk to Mom to see if I can smooth the way for him to come to dinner? Cody is the only guy here today. I'm sure he'd appreciate having a little more testosterone in the house."

"Mom will never go for it. She thinks Brad's a freak."

"Maybe if she got a chance to know him, she'd change her mind. Maybe she'd even let you date him."

Cassie appeared to be considering my idea. Of course if she went for it, I'd have to convince my straitlaced mother not only to allow Brad to come to dinner but to give him a fair shot as well.

"What do you have to lose?" I asked. "Sure, you can sneak out tonight, but then you'll be grounded when she finds out later, and Mom will *really* hate him. In the end, you won't be able to date him anyway. But if she winds up getting to know and like him..."

"Oh, all right. But this better work."

Somehow I got Mom to agree to let Brad come to dinner, and I enlisted Cody and Tara's help in smoothing over any rough spots in the conversation. I was simultaneously proud of myself for coming up with a good alternative to the situation and terrified the whole thing would blow up in my face if Mom really did hate Brad. As things turned out, the entire experience was one I'd always remember.

Later that evening I slid into the passenger seat of Cody's car and began to laugh hysterically. I couldn't help it. I had been holding it in all day. Not only had Mom allowed Brad to come to dinner but she had actually *liked* him.

"Did you see Cassie's face when Mom and Brad started talking about that conference they'd both attended?" I roared.

"She did seem to be a little upset," Cody agreed.

"And then when they began discussing books they both liked and the list was extensive?" I leaned back in the seat, holding my stomach. "I thought Cassie was going to get up and leave."

"The way her face turned red *was* kind of funny," Cody agreed as he pulled onto the highway.

"Poor Cassie thought she was dating a bad boy, but it turns out she's been lusting after an altar boy." I started laughing again.

"Okay, it's kind of funny, but it's not *that* funny." Cody glanced at me.

"I know." I drew in a deep breath as tears streamed down my face. "I really don't know why I can't stop laughing."

"Post traumatic stress? Temporary insanity? Too much wine?"

"Probably all of the above." I hiccuped as I tried to suppress my hysteria-induced giggles.

"I think you might need some fresh air," Cody teased. "Why don't we stop by to pick up Rambler and then head over to your place so you can change and get Max? Then we'll all go for a walk along the beach."

"I think that might be a very good idea."

Cody's suggestion about taking a walk along the beach was the best idea I'd heard all day. The summer crowds had gone, so it was just the two of us with the two dogs as they romped in the waves and we walked hand in hand along the shore. Cody had come to the island for a short visit in May in order to figure out what to do with his life. His most recent tour with the Navy had been drawing to a close and he'd needed to decide if he wanted to re-up or move on to something else. In the end he'd realized that he enjoyed spending time on the island where he grew up, with the people who had known him since childhood, so he'd resigned from the Navy and bought the newspaper the previous owner had decided to sell after moving away.

Cody had left after the Fourth of July in order to finish up with the Navy and to get his belongings out of storage. He'd moved back to the island a few days before Labor Day and began printing the newspaper a couple of weeks after that.

The two of us had a history I found to be embarrassing at the least. When Cody had returned in May, I'd thought our past would prevent us from ever being friends, but it turned out that after we'd worked on the first of three murders we'd solved together, any discomfort we'd felt had melted into our memories of the past.

During Cody's visit over the summer we'd settled into a comfortable friendship. When he'd left again I'd found I missed him (a lot), but since he'd returned I'd noticed that our relationship had settled into a sort of Neverland. I had feelings for him and it seemed he had feelings for me, but I knew our relationship was important to both of us, and neither he nor I seemed to be willing to risk the friendship we shared for the possibility of something more.

Still, I had no desire to date other men, and he didn't seem to have interest in dating other women, so we'd settled into a comfortable pairing the status of which was undefined but appeared to hold promise.

"It looks like it's going to be a busy week for both of us," I commented as the cold water washed over our bare feet.

"Yeah, it looks like it. I hoped to have something new and spectacular to report about Roxi's murder by the time the paper goes to print on Tuesday evening, but so far all I have is colorful confetti that appears to tell a story but isn't anywhere close to coming together."

"Maybe you'll get a break tomorrow," I offered.

"Maybe. I do have some leads I can follow up on. Maybe one of them will lead to another, and so on and so forth."

"I guess Beatrice hasn't been much help," I mused. "Which is odd, because the other cats Tansy sent to me started doing things right away. All Beatrice seems to do is eat and sleep."

"Are you sure the cat that was last seen sleeping on the back of your sofa is the one Bella said Tansy was sending? I mean, you do run a cat sanctuary. Isn't it possible someone just dropped her off on the night she showed up and the timing of her arrival caused you to believe she was Beatrice when actually she isn't?"

"I guess that's possible. But if it's true, where's Beatrice?"

"Did Bella give you any indication as to when you should expect her arrival?"

"Bella never really tells people anything. She just hints at stuff. But I don't remember her saying much at all about the cat, except that Beatrice would be by to help."

Max came running back to us with a huge stick in his mouth, which Rambler was trying his hardest to steal. I was happy to see Max having fun. The transition to my working every day had been hard on him.

"I've been a little worried about Max," I began.

"What's wrong with him?" Cody had a look of concern on his face.

"It's just that I've had to leave him home alone so often now that the bookstore is open. He's used to being with me most of the time. I was wondering if perhaps the newspaper could use a mascot?"

"You want me to bring Max to work with me?" Cody asked.

"It was a thought. He's well trained and I'm sure he wouldn't be a bother. I'd take him to the bookstore, but I can't have him on the side where we sell food, and I'm afraid if I left him in the lounge he'd divert attention away from the cats we're trying to find homes for. He really will just lie by your desk while you're working, and if you need to go out he loves to ride in the car."

Cody shrugged. "Yeah, okay. We can try it out. And on the days it doesn't work for me to take him with me I'm sure Mr. Parsons would be happy to let him hang out at the house with him and Rambler."

I stood on tiptoe, threw my arms around Cody's neck, and kissed him on the cheek. "Thank you so much. Max thanks you too."

Cody smiled. "If I knew the secret to your sweet kisses was through Max, I would have offered to have him tag along with me a long time ago. What do I get if I take Beatrice as well?"

"Don't push it." I grinned.

Cody stopped walking. We stood side by side and looked out over the gently rolling waves. It was a beautiful night with a clear and starry sky. The air had chilled, but we were wearing heavy sweatshirts and there was no wind.

"I'm a little worried about Destiny," I told Cody. I filled him in on my conversation with Tara.

Cody frowned. "I can see how the situation would be difficult. Destiny has never been easy to deal with, and now with all the pregnancy hormones thrown in . . ."

"I feel bad for everyone involved and really want to help, but I also don't want to make it worse. I thought I might try talking to her. She needs a friend. We've known each other her whole life, and while I may not be that much older than she is, I think I'm enough older that she might view me as an adult who can help."

"I think you should talk to her. Just be prepared if she comes at you with claws bared before you can get a word out."

"I'll wear long sleeves," I promised.

I leaned my head on Cody's shoulder as we continued to stroll. It really was the perfect autumn evening. I couldn't remember the last time I'd felt quite so content.

"I really missed this when I was away," Cody said.

"The ocean? You were in the Navy. Didn't you see plenty of ocean?"

"I saw far too much ocean, but that isn't what I meant. I missed having a home and feeling part of a community. I missed Sunday dinners at your mom's and quiet walks on the beach at the end of the day." Cody turned and looked at me. "And most of all I missed you."

I smiled. "Yeah?"

"Yeah."

"So I was wondering if you were planning to attend the ball on Saturday."

"I thought about it. Are you going?" Cody asked.

"I probably will. It is, after all, a fund-raiser for the island, and I know the committee is encouraging everyone to buy a ticket."

"Do you think we should ride there together?"

"There's really limited parking," I said. "It might be a good idea to carpool."

"Perhaps I can pick you up around seven?"

"Seven is good." I smiled. "You'll need a costume."

"A mask isn't enough?" Cody asked.

"Technically it is. A lot of men just wear their regular Sunday suits with a black mask. But there are those who dress a bit more elaborately. I think Aunt Maggie is going as Marie Antoinette."

"Did you have something in mind?" Cody queried.

"Last year I wore a period costume."

"Which period?"

I found myself blushing, although I had no idea why. "I went as Cleopatra."

Cody raised his eyebrows. "Really? It sounds like a costume I'd like to see. Perhaps I should dress as Marc Antony?"

I shrugged. "If you'd like. Don't forget the mask."

Chapter 6

Monday, September 21

I woke the following morning to the sound of rain hitting the roof above my head. I leaned up on one elbow and looked out the window toward the sea. All I could see was a thick bank of fog, which had apparently accompanied the rain.

"Guess we won't get our run in this morning," I said to Max, who looked up from his spot at the foot of my bed. He looked at the fog and lay back down. At least I supposed he looked at the fog. To be honest, I don't really know what he was looking at.

"I know you're bummed that we won't be able to take a run, but at least I arranged for you to go sleuthing with Cody, so you won't have to stay home all by yourself. That will be nice. Don't you think?"

Max thumped his tail one time in a halfhearted show of appreciation.

Beatrice must have realized it was time to get up because she crawled out from under the covers and began doing the kitty yoga she had performed each morning since she'd been with me. Downward dog, into cat pose, and finally cobra.

I tossed back the covers and slid my legs over the side of the bed. I winced as my shoulder, stiff from sleeping on it, reminded me what a klutz I had been the previous day. I pulled a long sweatshirt over the boxer shorts and tank I wore to bed and slipped my feet into knee-high slippers. I made my way downstairs, opened the side door to let Max out, and then tossed a match on the fire. I turned on the coffeemaker and filled Beatrice's food and water dishes.

By the time the coffee was made Max was back from his morning romp, so I dried him off with an old towel and then fed him as well. I grabbed the coffee I had poured into my Coffee Cat Books mug, then wandered over to the sofa, where I pulled one of Maggie's quilts over my lap. I felt myself relax into the serenity of the morning as I watched the dancing of the flames in the fireplace.

I took a slow sip of my coffee as I listened to the sound of the rain compete with the crashing of the waves. Early morning, before the urgency of the day could invade, was usually my favorite time.

Beatrice finished her breakfast and then joined me on the sofa, curling up in my lap and beginning to purr.

"Are you settling in for a nap already?" I asked the furry feline. "We just got up."

Beatrice closed her eyes and proceeded to ignore me.

"Is your name even Beatrice?" I asked.

I was pretty sure her purrs had turned to snores.

"I don't mean to be pushy, but if Tansy sent you to help shouldn't you be doing something?"

Max trotted into the room and lay down in front of the fire, watching me as I attempted to communicate with the lazy cat. I leaned over to look at her face. She was definitely sleeping. I looked at Max. "I don't suppose you have any ideas?"

Max buried his face in his paws.

I took another sip of my coffee, then leaned my head back against the sofa. Between the steady drumming of the rain and the warmth from the fire, I found that, like Beatrice, I was fading away into the land of dreams. I'm not sure how long I slept, but I must have, because the next thing I knew a voice in the distance was pulling me away from a dream I didn't particularly want to leave.

"Cait."

I resisted the interruption as my dream lover's arms pulled me into his embrace. Lips that I found unable to resist were inches from mine as someone outside my dream began to shake my shoulder.

"Cait. Wake up, honey."

Cody's image began to fade into the fog. I reached for him, but I could feel myself being pulled from my dream state. I wanted to yell at whoever was waking me up to go away, but I realized it was too late.

I felt something brush my cheek as the voice called to me again.

"Cait. It's eight thirty. We're both going to be late if you don't wake up."

"Cody?" I managed to open my eyes just a crack.

"I came for Max."

"I was dreaming about you." I tried to sit up straight.

"Dreaming about me?" Cody grinned.

"Not like that." Suddenly, I was completely awake.

Cody handed me a tissue.

"I'm not crying."

"You have a little drool." He pointed to the corner of his mouth.

I groaned. This wasn't how I wanted to start my day.

I set Beatrice to the side and sat up straight.

"You're really adorable when you sleep, drool and all."

"Bite me."

"And cheerful in the mornings to boot."

I glared at the man who looked too good to be real.

"I really do need to get going and I thought I overheard you promise Tara you would be in by nine. Not that you don't look adorable, but you might want to catch a quick shower."

I groaned as I ran my hand through the rat's nest on top of my head.

"How did you get in here?" I asked as Cody turned to leave.

"The door was open. I knocked, but you didn't answer, so I came in. Call me later. Maybe we can catch lunch."

And with that the man of my dreams was gone.

"I'm so sorry I'm late," I apologized as I ran in through the front door of Coffee Cat Books at nine thirty.

"It's okay," Tara said. "With all the rain, we haven't had a single customer. Do you need help with the cats?"

I looked out at the sheets of rain falling from the sky. "No, I've got it. I'm already wet. Grab the door so I can bring each crate directly inside. The cats weren't happy with the rain when they were transferred into the car, and I don't think they're going to be any happier when I bring them inside."

After I brought all four crates in I settled the slightly drenched felines into the cat lounge, where Tara had already built a roaring fire. It was warm and cozy and exactly the kind of place I would want to spend a rainy day, reading a good book, sipping a specially blended latte, and curling up with one of our cats.

"I wonder if we'll get any foot traffic today." The rain seemed to have increased in intensity since I'd been in town.

"The ferries are running. I checked. Whether anyone will bother to take a ferry over for a day of shopping and relaxation is doubtful. I thought we'd close early if things haven't picked up by noon. We have enough chores to keep us occupied for a few hours."

"Chores?" I asked.

"Dusting, sweeping, paying bills."

"I'll clean and you can pay the bills." I poured myself a cup of coffee from the pot. Hopefully this one wouldn't put me to sleep.

"We need to make a decision about whether to reorder inventory," Tara commented as I wrapped my hands around the warm mug. "We have some money in savings, but we're headed into winter and things will slow down and our mortgage payments and utilities will still need to be paid."

"What do you think?" If I knew Tara—and I did—she'd already made up her mind about what to do and was only asking me so I would feel included.

"I think we should hold off on novelty items for sure," she began. "As for the books, we'll want to keep up with the delivery of new releases each month, but maybe we should order half as many."

"We can always special order more if we run out."

"We can. And we will. As far as the coffee bar goes, we'll want to keep the basic supplies on hand, but we'll need to be careful about not ordering too many specialty items. We can create a winter menu to adjust for the specialty drinks if we need to."

"Sounds good to me."

Tara set her laptop on one of the tables near the window. I watched as she studied the screen in front of her. I really was glad she was in charge of the paperwork. It's not that I couldn't have done it; it was more that I wouldn't have wanted to.

Dusting is boring, but it's also mindless work that allows you to think about other things while you're preforming the task. Things like handsome images in a foggy sea. I didn't remember a lot about the dream Cody woke me from, but I was pretty sure I was lost in a fog when strong arms—his strong arms—had reached out to guide me. I wasn't sure what the dream meant—most likely nothing—but I couldn't help but want to return to the sense of safety I'd felt in his embrace.

"What are you smiling about?" Tara asked.

"Smiling?"

"You've been standing there with a huge grin on your face for at least two minutes. What's on your mind?"

"It's 'Too Good to Be Legal' night on *Cooking With Cathy* tonight," I improvised. "I was just imagining the yummy choices we're going to have. Let's not forget to stop by the market before we head out to the cabin."

"I'll print off a list of ingredients," Tara offered as she headed toward the office.

I returned to my dusting. Somehow the brief conversation I'd had with Tara had suppressed the memory of the dream I'd been having before she interrupted. Oh, well; mooning over Cody West was going to lead to no good anyway.

I knelt down on the floor to work on the lowest shelf. Not that most people would notice a little dust all the way down there, but Tara was a stickler for cleanliness. Even when we were kids, her room had been spotless, while mine had been anything but.

I was leaning back to stretch out my lower back when I heard the bell over the door announce a customer. I stood up from behind the bookshelf and greeted our new arrival: Becky Wood.

"Morning, Becky. Heck of a day to be out shopping."

"Trust me, the main thing on my mind at this moment is curling up in front of the fire with a good book and a cup of hot coffee. Unfortunately, I'm out of new reading material. I'm also out of coffee, so I figured I'd risk getting wet and come in for both."

"I can make you a coffee while you browse. What'll you have?"

"Just a black coffee is fine. I'm trying to lose a few pounds."

Becky wasn't fat, but if what I'd heard about her husband, Trace, having a wandering eye was true, I guess I couldn't blame her for wanting to firm up a bit.

"I guess you heard about Roxi Pettigrew," I fished. Trish had indicated that Trace was one of the men Roxi had been seen fooling around with.

Becky's expression tightened. "I heard. Can't say I'm overly upset about it."

"You didn't get along with Roxi?" I handed Becky her cup of coffee.

"We used to be friends until she started getting along with men who weren't hers to get along with."

"Yeah, I'd heard something like that. Guess I can see why there are those who are just as happy to see her dead."

Becky paused and then sighed. "It's not so much that I'm glad she's dead. It's just that I'm glad she isn't here."

I pretended to dust a shelf I'd already dusted so I could position myself near where she was browsing.

"Do you think Roxi's tendency to flirt might have gotten her killed?"

I watched Becky's face as she answered. "Maybe." She shrugged. "I know I wanted to strangle her, and quite honestly, I might have done it if I hadn't heard she was moving at the end of the month."

"Moving?" I asked.

"Yeah. Trace told me she'd sold Jimmy's boat and was leaving the island for good."

"I hadn't heard that," I admitted.

"I don't think she was telling folks yet. Trace told me that she didn't want people talking about it until she was ready to quit her job at the diner. I suppose that makes sense. Things can get awkward once you give notice at your job. Especially after everything Ernie did for her."

"I heard he gave her a month off with pay."

"He did more than that. He gave her the month off and he also paid off some big debt Jimmy had when he died. Sounded like it was a boatload of money."

"I hadn't heard about a debt either. I guess you should be the amateur sleuth," I buttered her up for the string of questions I suddenly had.

Becky smiled. "You think I could be a detective?"

"You seem to know more than most about what's going on," I continued. "I don't suppose you know what sort of debt Jimmy left behind."

"I'm pretty sure it had to do with a business deal of some sort he got pulled into."

"Any idea who he was in debt to?" I asked.

"No. Trace didn't say and I didn't ask. I was more concerned with making sure Trace knew it could be bad for his health if he kept providing a shoulder for Roxi to cry on. I mean, I get that it's a terrible thing to lose a husband and to be left with a whole pile of problems, but the girl had no right to turn to *my* husband in her time of need. You know what I mean?"

"Yeah, I get why you'd be upset."

Becky pulled a book off the shelf, turned it over, and read the back cover. She frowned and then replaced it. "I'm looking for a really good mystery romance. Can you recommend anything?"

"We have a couple of really popular ones on the display table in the front."

Becky walked away, effectively ending the conversation, but that was okay. She had given me a few things to follow up on. I remembered Cody had mentioned meeting for lunch, and I planned to suggest we go to the Driftwood, where we could talk to Ernie about the debt he'd paid off while we ate.

The heavy rain continued as the morning wore on. Tara and I decided there was no use staying open; Becky had been the only customer we'd had all day, so she decided to take some of the paperwork she had been trying to catch up on home with her and I decided to pay a visit to Roxi's best friend Stacy. Because today was Monday, Tara arranged to meet me at the cabin later in the day for *Cooking With Cathy*.

Stacy worked at the local thrift store. Luckily, she was alone in the store when I arrived. It appeared as if the entire town of Pelican Bay was deserted, most likely due to the storm.

"Cait, I'm so glad you stopped in," Stacy greeted me. "You're the first customer I've had all day."

"Yeah, it's pretty dead out there. We closed the bookstore. Maybe you should do the same. I doubt anyone is going to be out shopping in this weather."

"I'd love to close, but unlike you, I'm just an employee, not an owner, so it isn't up to me. What can I get for you?"

"Actually, I'm just here to ask about Roxi."

"Figured you'd be working with Finn again. I don't know if I can add anything to what I've already told him, though."

"Do you happen to know what it was Jimmy got himself involved in before he died?"

Stacy frowned. "Not really. All I know is that Roxi was concerned about some business deal Jimmy had become involved in. He was pretty vague about exactly what it was, which made her really uncomfortable, but he assured her that he was going to make a bunch of money in a short amount of time and they could finally fix their boat. You heard his winch blew up and his engine was on its last leg?"

"Yeah, I heard."

"Anyway, after the car accident a man showed up and informed Roxi that Jimmy had twenty thousand dollars that didn't belong to him. She insisted that she didn't know anything about any twenty grand and she certainly didn't have it, but the guy didn't seem to care. He just told her that she'd better find a way to come up with it or bad things were going to come her way. Roxi was scared to death of this guy, and I know she tried everything she could think of to get the money."

"Do you think the guy who was trying to collect the twenty grand is the one who killed her?" I asked.

"Honestly, I have no idea."

"Did you know Roxi sold Jimmy's boat and planned to move at the end of the month?"

"What? No, she never said anything about moving. Are you sure?"

"No, I'm not sure. Becky Wood told me that's what Trace told her."

"I know Roxi and Trace were messing around. I'm pretty sure he gave her some money. In fact, I'm pretty sure there were several men on the island who gave Roxi money in the past couple of months. Roxi was my best friend and I cared about her, but I feel like there was something going on that she wasn't telling me about."

"What do you mean?" I asked.

"I don't know exactly. Roxi just seemed different the last couple of weeks before she died. She said everything was fine, but I knew her well enough to tell she was hiding something. I just wish I'd tried harder to figure out what that something was."

Chapter 7

"Your cat has been sitting staring out the window ever since I've been here," Tara commented later that evening as she poured nuts into the chocolate. "It's almost like she's looking for something, or maybe waiting for someone."

I glanced at Beatrice. She had been peering intently at something for the past hour in spite of the fact that it was still raining and there really wasn't anything to see. Still, I did hope she knew something I didn't. To be honest, I kept waiting for her to do something, anything that might point us in a direction. Bella had said Beatrice would take me where I needed to go, but so far she hadn't taken me any farther than the sofa.

"Maybe she's getting ready to make her move, whatever that might be," I said. "At this point Cody and I need all the help we can get."

"Have you talked to Finn?" Tara asked.

"We stopped in to chat with him after we had lunch. He said he had a few ideas he was looking in to, but he declined to offer specifics. I think he's as stumped as we are."

"And Ernie didn't know anything?" Tara began measuring the flour she would need to add to the first layer of the caramel brownies we were making. We were cooking along with Cathy, though we both seemed to be too distracted to pay much attention to the banter portion of the show tonight.

"Not really. He did confirm that Jimmy left Roxi with a debt she was unable to pay. He didn't know the total amount or who it was owed to, but he did share that Roxi came to work one day maybe six weeks ago with a black eye. At first she claimed she'd run into an open cabinet door, but she later admitted that Jimmy had gotten into debt to some bad men who were intent on collecting despite the fact that Jimmy was dead. Ernie said he gave her five thousand dollars, but he didn't think it was enough to get her out of the hole completely. Ernie believes Roxi died as a result of her inability to pay the remainder, but Finn doesn't agree."

"No?" Tara poured the batter she'd been mixing into a casserole dish. "Why not?"

"He told us it seemed obvious that whoever killed Roxi and then buried her in her own grave was trying to hide the body. He said most of the time back-alley money lenders trying to collect a debt look to make a statement by displaying the body in a public place, where it can serve as a warning to others who may be behind on their payments."

"I guess that makes sense."

"Besides, Stacy indicated that the total amount of the debt was twenty grand. We know Ernie gave Roxi five, and Stacy thought there were others who gave her money as well. It seems like a money lender would have a bit more patience if Roxi was making payments."

"Yeah, I have to agree. And now that Roxi is dead the guy has no way to collect the balance. Did you preheat the oven?" Tara asked.

I nodded.

"Knowing that Jimmy owed these less-than-law-abiding citizens a chunk of cash makes me wonder if his accident was really an accident at all," Tara mused.

"Finn said the same thing. He's taking another look at Jimmy's accident."

"Let's start gathering the ingredients for the casserole while the dessert bakes," Tara suggested. "What time are the guys getting here?"

"Should be any minute now. In fact, I thought Danny would be here by now because I know he didn't have any tours today. I expected to find him camped out here when I got home. He usually doesn't stay on the boat when it's storming."

"Maybe he stopped off over at O'Malley's," Tara offered.

I shrugged. "I guess he might have."

I began grating the first of the three types of cheese we planned to use.

"So how do you think it's working out for all of us now that Coffee Cat Books has officially taken over the scheduling for Danny?" Tara asked.

"I don't know. I guess it's working out okay. Why do you ask?"

Tara put a pan of water on the stove to boil. "Danny is very disorganized."

"Yeah, so? He's always been disorganized."

"Maybe, but I guess I hadn't realized just how bad it was until we started scheduling for him full-time. I'm afraid his lack of follow-through is not only going to negatively affect Hart of the Sea Tours but Coffee Cat Books as well."

I stopped what I was doing to look directly at Tara. "What do you mean?"

"Visitors come to us to book their tours. We're the face they see and will remember if something goes wrong. Danny messed up the start time on two tours in the past two weeks. In both of those instances it was simply because he didn't bother to check his messages, and in both cases it was me who had to listen to the customer complain. I think if we're going to continue to do this for Danny you need to talk to him."

"Me? Why me?"

"He's your brother. Besides, I've tried to talk to him and he just blows me off. If he can't get his act together I really think we should tell him that we can no longer handle his scheduling."

I took a deep breath. Tara was right; Danny wasn't all that good about checking his messages on a regular basis and he did tend to miss important updates about the tours that were scheduled. But he'd only messed up the start time on two tours since we'd been handling the scheduling for him, and in both cases the groups who had booked charters had ended up compensated and happy.

I suspected the tension between Tara and Danny had to do with more than two messed-up charters. The fact that Tara happened to bring the whole thing up on the heels of her suggesting that Danny might be hanging out at O'Malley's seemed as good an indicator as any that she was having a hard time really letting go of Danny even though they'd come to an agreement about it.

"Okay, I'll talk to him," I agreed.

"Thank you. And be firm."

"I'll try. And as long as we're on the subject of schedules, I have other news."

Tara looked at me with suspicion in her eye. I couldn't really blame her. I hadn't been the most reliable partner. "What kind of news?"

"Bitzy has decided to take some time for herself now that her husband has officially left her for another woman and everyone knows about it, and I was asked to take over the Tuesday and Thursday cardio classes. At least temporarily."

Tara frowned. "Are you going to?"

"I don't know. I wanted to talk to you before I decided. I hate to see the class just dissolve, and I know that's exactly what will happen if they can't find a replacement. But I know that taking the class is something we decided to do together. If I teach I'm afraid it might not be as much fun for you."

"Half the fun *was* hiding out in the back of the room together complaining about Bitzy," Tara admitted.

"Exactly. The other problem is that if I'm teaching I won't be able to cut out of class early like we've been doing to open the store on time."

Tara bit her lip as she poured the pasta into the boiling water. I know how she likes to think each and every decision through as if it might be the most important of her life.

"We already discussed opening later over the winter," Tara began, "so I don't think not being able to leave early will be a problem. And I have to admit it won't be as fun without you to complain to, but I also hate to see the class end, so I think you should do it. When would you start?"

"Tomorrow."

"Then I guess I'd better figure out a new buddy to hang back and complain about you with."

I hugged Tara. "Thanks. I think I'd like to try this."

The lights in the cabin flickered as thunder sounded in the distance. I hoped the electricity wouldn't go out before we finished making the delicious meal we were preparing or we'd be serving peanut butter and jelly sandwiches for dinner.

"It looks like Cody just pulled into the drive," Tara said.

I went to the door and opened it as first Max and then Cody came trotting in.

"It's really coming down out there," he said as he shook the rain from his jacket and then hung it up to dry. "I hope we don't end up with flooding in the low-lying areas."

"But if we do you'll end up with an additional story for the midweek edition of the paper," I pointed out as I dried Max and then filled his food and water dishes.

"True. It's odd, though, when you start to look at everything that occurs on the island, good or bad, as a potential story."

Cody opened the refrigerator and took out a beer. "Danny's not here?"

"No, not yet," I answered. "Did you and Max dig up any new leads today?"

"Maybe one of us should call Danny to see if he's still planning to come for dinner," Tara said. "The casserole is almost done."

"I'll call him," I offered. I let the phone ring until the answering machine came on and then left a message.

"If he isn't here by the time the food is done we'll start without him," I decided.

"It'll be his loss," Cody said. "It smells wonderful in here."

"We made a bunch. If Danny doesn't show we'll have a ton left. Why don't you take some to Mr. Parsons?" I suggested.

"I'm sure he'd enjoy that. I thought about asking him if he wanted to come along tonight, but he mentioned that Banjo and Summer were going to stop by this evening. They're bringing Chinese food to go with the soap opera marathon they have planned."

"It's odd the way they watch those old tapes over and over again," I commented.

"I have to admit they're kind of addicting," Cody said. "I'd never even seen a soap opera prior to moving in with Mr. Parsons, but now I find I quite enjoy them."

"Oh, brother," I groaned.

"It's really no different than—" Cody began but was interrupted when his cell phone rang.

"Is it Danny?" Tara asked.

"Finn." Cody answered the call. "Hey, what's up?"

I watched Cody's face as he listened to whatever Finn was telling him. He was frowning.

"Okay, thanks," he said.

"What is it?" I asked after he hung up, hoping the call hadn't been bad news about Danny.

"Brianna Sommers called Finn in hysterics. It seems she found out that Tony had not only been spending time with Roxi before she died but he gave her their entire life savings. Brianna freaked out and threw a vase at his head. It knocked him out."

"Is he okay?"

"His head wound was severe enough that he's having him airlifted to the hospital in Seattle. Brianna is a total mess and Finn's afraid that if she doesn't get a grip she could hurt the baby. He wants me to go over to her place to help calm her down while he deals with arranging for the medevac."

"Why you?" I asked.

"Brianna is asking for me."

I knew Cody and Brianna had dated in high school. I guess I could see why she might turn to him now.

"If you need anything don't hesitate to call," I offered. "Brianna has to be eight months along. I hope she doesn't go into labor."

"Yeah, me too." Cody kissed me on the cheek. "I'll call you later."

Chapter 8

Tuesday, September 22

I woke to sunshine the following morning. I wanted to get to the community center early to set up for the class, so Tara had decided to just meet me there. I hoped she'd come. I knew that if it weren't for the fact that I picked her up every Tuesday and Thursday morning, she most likely would have stopped coming to class months ago. Tara isn't a fan of sweat and sore muscles, so more often than not she tends to remain exercise adverse, while I love to dive right into the thick of things.

I plugged my iPod into the docking station and adjusted the volume on the sound system. Luckily, Tara realized I was most likely going to need my own music, so she'd helped me put together a playlist we knew the ladies who frequented the class would enjoy. I wanted to add my own twist to the class, so I'd added a few new songs as well.

"Bitzy not here?" a woman I always thought of as Pink Headband asked.

"No. She's taking some time off, so I'm subbing for the time being."

"Guess I'm not surprised she decided to lay low for a while," the woman responded. "I heard her soon-to-be ex is already engaged to his new girlfriend. You'd think the guy would wait until the divorce was final to put a ring on the lady's finger."

"I heard the girlfriend is pregnant," another woman in the group, who I identify as Stuck in the Eighties Leg Warmers, commented. "In fact, I'm pretty sure she was already prego before Bitzy even knew her lowlife husband was cheating on her."

"Poor Bitzy. I hadn't heard all of that." I began handing out mats for the floor exercises.

"If you ask me, this whole island seems to be suffering from an outbreak of premature-death-due-to-cheating fever," Pink Headband replied. "First Keith and now Roxi. I wouldn't be a bit surprised if Bitzy's cheating husband is the next corpse to show up in some random location."

I looked more closely at Pink Headband. The way she'd made the statement sounded almost like a threat. While I knew she had been taking classes with Bitzy for a number of years, her comment seemed to contain more venom than a mere acquaintance would make.

"Are you and Bitzy close?" I asked.

The woman shrugged. "Not really. I just know what it's like to have a man you thought you trusted cheat on you."

"I guess that would be difficult." I waved to Tara who, thankfully, had just walked in and was setting up in the back. "But I doubt he'll end up a victim. I heard Bitzy's husband left the area with the new girlfriend."

"He's back," Stuck in the Eighties informed me.

That was news to me. No wonder Bitzy was lying low.

"I guess you all heard Brianna Sommers tried to kill her cheater of a husband," Pink Headband announced.

"I don't think she intentionally tried to kill him," I countered. "I think she just got angry and threw something at him. Unfortunately, the something she threw was heavy and it hit him in just the right spot to cause a pretty serious injury."

Cody had called later last night to say that both Tony and Brianna ended up being hospitalized. His head wound was pretty serious and she had to be sedated in order to calm her down. Given her advanced state of pregnancy, the doctor wanted to keep her in the hospital to monitor the situation.

"I wouldn't blame Brianna if she *had* intentionally tried to kill the jerk," Stuck in the Eighties insisted. "Doris Rutherford told me that not only did Tony give Roxi the five grand that he and Brianna had been saving to take a trip to visit her parents after the baby was born but he'd given her the ten grand Brianna's grandmother left her."

"Are we going to start soon?" Yellow Sweatpants asked. "I have an appointment right after class."

I looked at the clock. We should have started five minutes ago. "I'm ready now. Let's start with some stretching." I clicked on the music and began my routine.

When I pulled up in front of Coffee Cat Books after leaving the community center I noticed Destiny sitting in the passenger waiting area for the ferry. There was a backpack on the ground next to her and her face bore such a look of hopelessness that I decided to go over to talk to her before heading into the store. She'd most likely tell me to get lost, but I felt I had to try.

"It's a beautiful day," I said as I looked up toward the bright sun that was framed with a crystal-clear sky.

Destiny didn't respond, continuing to stare blankly into the distance.

"Are you going somewhere?" I asked.

"I'm waitin' for the ferry, ain't I?"

"Yes, I suppose you are. It's a nice day to be on the water. If I didn't have to work I might take a ride over to one of the other islands as well. Best keep an eye on the time, though. They cut the last ferry for the winter, so if you miss the five o'clock you're going to be stuck wherever it is you're going until tomorrow."

Destiny shrugged. "Ain't coming back."

"You're staying over?"

"I'm headin' out for good."

I frowned. "I see. Does your mom know about this?"

"I left a note." Destiny folded her hands in her lap and stared down at the wooden decking on the wharf.

"I'm sure she'll want to have a chance to speak to you before you go. Maybe you should wait to leave until you can tell her good-bye in person. I'm sure she's going to miss you very much."

"She'll be glad I'm gone."

"Oh, I doubt that. You're her daughter and she loves you."

Destiny looked up and stared me straight in the eye. I could see she firmly believed what she was about to share. "She thinks I'm a problem. She's worried I'm a bad influence on Serenity and Trinity. When she gets my note she'll be glad I'm out of her hair."

A sixteen-year-old girl out in the world on her own was never a good thing. A pregnant sixteen-year-old was something I couldn't allow to happen. I knew I had to stop her; I just needed to figure out how to do it. Sure, I could physically restrain her and call her mother to come get her, but she'd just run away again. I needed a better solution and I needed it fast.

"As long as you're heading out anyway, maybe you can do me a favor."

Destiny looked at me suspiciously. "What kind of favor?"

"I was going to have to go to the mainland on Saturday to deliver a kitten that's been adopted by a family in Seattle, but I'm really too busy. If you're going to the mainland anyway, perhaps you can wait until Saturday and take the kitten with you. I'll pay you," I added when I could see she was about to turn me down.

"How much?" Destiny asked.

"Two hundred dollars."

Destiny's eyes grew wide. I could tell she was considering it. "Two fifty and I take the kitten today."

"Three hundred and you wait until Saturday."

Destiny dropped her eyes. "Then I have to say no. I ain't going home. Not even for a few days."

"How about if I let you stay with me until Saturday?" I tried.

Destiny frowned. "This ain't no trick, is it? You aren't just goin' to make me miss the last ferry out for the day and then send me home?"

"It's not a trick, but I will need to call your mom to tell her you're going to be staying with me. I wouldn't want her to worry."

Destiny bit her lip. "I don't know. What if she tries to stop me from leavin'?"

"I thought you said she'd be glad you were going," I reminded her.

"Yeah." The girl who suddenly looked a lot younger than sixteen twisted a lock of her long hair around her finger. "She will be." She looked me directly in the eye for the first time. "Five hundred dollars."

The girl knew how to play hardball.

"Five hundred dollars, but you help Tara and me in the store until you leave."

"Deal."

Now all I had to do was tell Tara I'd found us some part-time help we probably didn't need in the juvenile delinquent department.

"Look who's coming from the ferry," Tara commented after I'd filled her in and we'd set Destiny to restocking the supplies in the coffee bar.

I looked toward the ferry to see our dark stranger departing. "But it's not Saturday. He always comes on Saturday."

Tara shrugged. "I guess he had business on the island today."

As he did every time the man arrived on the island, the black and white cat who seemed to be in some way attached to him appeared.

"I'm going to follow him," I informed Tara. "From a distance of course, so as to be inconspicuous. It's not that busy today, so you should be fine without me for a few minutes."

Tara didn't look thrilled with my desertion, but she didn't argue. I casually stepped out of the bookstore once the man and the cat had passed and followed them from a safe distance. The man never turned around, but I sensed the cat knew I was there.

The man turned the corner where the wharf met Main Street and walked briskly down the sidewalk. I followed him past Herbalities, Ship Wreck, Off the Hook, the Bait and Stitch, and For the Halibut. I closed the distance between us when he turned the corner onto Harbor Boulevard and disappeared. I mean, he literally disappeared. He hadn't been that far ahead of me, so there was no way he could have made it to the next intersection before I turned onto Harbor, so the only explanation was that he had slipped into one of the retail establishments on that first block.

On the corner of Harbor and Main was the Driftwood Café, a popular place with the lunch crowd. Although it was just after eleven, it was crowded with weekday diners. It wasn't all that large, however, so a quick look inside confirmed what I suspected: neither man nor cat was in sight.

"Did you see a tall elderly man with pale skin wearing a black suit and hat come in here in the past minute?" I asked Molly Quinby, the cashier and hostess. Molly had lived on the island her entire life, as I had lived here for mine, so the two of us were well acquainted.

"No. I haven't seen anyone like that come in today or any other day, although I've seen a man fitting that description walk by in the past. Usually on Saturdays."

"Was he with anyone on any of those occasions?" I asked.

"Not a soul. Although there did appear to be a cat following him. Do you need a table?"

"No, not today." I thanked her for the information and headed back out onto the sidewalk.

Next to the Driftwood was a building that had been subdivided into four smaller spaces, including the *Madrona Island News* office, the sheriff's office, the post office, and the Madrona Island library. The post office was closed, as it was every day between eleven and twelve thirty, while the postmaster went home for lunch. The sheriff's office was likewise dark. There was a sign in the window of the newspaper, announcing that Cody was delivering papers and would be back soon.

I slipped into the library, which was open, and made my way to the front desk.

"Did you see a tall elderly man with pale skin dressed in a black suit and hat who might have been followed by a cat come through here?" I asked the volunteer who was working the counter.

"I haven't seen anyone fitting that description and we don't allow animals, so I would have noticed the cat."

"Do you ever volunteer on Saturdays?" I asked.

"Usually. Why?"

"Have you ever seen a man who looks like that in here on a Saturday?"

She shook her head. "No, and I'm sure I would remember him. Who wears a suit on Madrona Island?"

The volunteer had a point. Madrona Island was known for its casual approach to both life and attire. Other than weddings or funerals, you rarely saw a man dressed in a suit.

"Although," the woman added, "I do remember seeing a man in a dark suit two or three weeks ago. I was on my way back to the island from the mainland, where I'd been visiting a friend, and we came over on the same ferry."

"Was it the eleven o'clock Saturday ferry?" I wondered.

"Actually, it was. I arranged to start my shift at noon that day. The only reason I remember seeing the guy is because he was acting sort of odd."

I leaned my elbows on the counter and leaned forward. I lowered my voice so as not to be overheard. "Odd how?" I asked.

She narrowed her brow as she seemed to consider my question. "For one thing, he not only never spoke to anyone but he almost didn't seem aware of anyone. He just sat there staring into space. It was a beautiful day and almost everyone was either out on the deck or sitting near the windows, enjoying the view, but he just looked straight ahead. It's not like I spent the whole trip looking at the guy, but when I did look in his direction, he not only never made eye contact with anyone he never changed his facial expression. It was like he was made of wax."

"Did you notice him doing anything at all?"

The woman screwed up her face as she formed an answer. "No, I don't think so. The guy had on these really dark glasses, and as far as I can remember, he never removed them the entire time he was on the ferry. I remember wondering if he was asleep behind those glasses."

"I guess he could have been."

She shrugged. "Yeah, I guess, although he was sitting pretty rigidly and he didn't look very comfortable."

I glanced around the room. There weren't a lot of patrons in the library, and the checkout desk faced the door, so there was little chance the man could have ducked in and hid between the stacks. I was trying to make up my mind whether to have a look for myself when the woman spoke again.

"You're one of the owners of the new bookstore," the library volunteer said. "I've been trying to remember where I've seen you."

"Yeah, I'm Cait."

"I'm Angie. I just moved to the island in April. I've been meaning to come in to check things out. I guess you can tell by my choice of Saturday activity that I love books."

"Please do stop by when you have a chance. My partner's name is Tara. Either of us would be happy to show you around. We have a coffee bar and a cat lounge as well, if you like coffee and cats."

"Thanks, I'll do that. I'm not much of a coffee drinker and I really don't care for cats, but I love books."

"Are you a member of the Mystery Lovers Book Club?"

"Yeah. How'd you know?"

"Cody West mentioned to me that he spoke to someone named Angie from the library about Roxi Pettigrew's death."

"Yeah, that was me. I'm still having a hard time believing what everyone's saying about her. She seemed so nice. In fact, she was the one who told me about the book club. We volunteer at the church together on Tuesdays. The kids loved her. Everyone there was pretty upset by what happened to her."

"Do you know why anyone would want to hurt her?" I asked.

Angie shrugged. "Not really. I know she had a problem she was working through. We really weren't close enough for her to confide in me, but I could tell she was dealing with some heavy stuff. And it seemed like it was more than just the loss of her husband, although that would be enough in and of itself to send most people into emotional turmoil. I can't imagine how hard it must have been for her to try to get on with her life."

"Did she ever say anything to you about needing money?"

Angie frowned. "Not really, although she did say something about someone giving her money once. I remember she was late for our group at the church maybe a month ago, and she mentioned that she had to go to the bank to deposit some money that one of her friends had given her."

"Did she say which friend?"

Angie bit her lip as she appeared to be considering my question. "I think she said the friend who gave her the money was named Greg."

Greg Westlake, I realized. As unlikely as it seemed, maybe Greg and Roxi really did have a thing going on. He didn't seem to be Roxi's type at all, but if she needed money and he had it...

I chatted with the woman for a few more minutes, then returned to the sidewalk and looked up and down the street. The man was nowhere in sight. The only thing to do was to return to the bookstore.

"The guy totally vanished," I informed Tara as soon as I got there.

"What do you mean, he vanished?" Tara asked.

"I was following him just fine until he turned on to Harbor. I followed him around the corner, but he was gone. I wasn't that far behind. There was no way he made it to Second Street, so I figured he'd slipped into one of the buildings between Main and there, but I didn't find him in any of the places that were open."

"He can't have just vanished."

"Apparently he did, despite what common sense would dictate. Where's Destiny?" I noticed for the first time that the girl wasn't around.

"Her mom came by on her lunch hour. They went out to talk, but she said she'd bring Destiny by after. As far as I could tell by the brief exchange I overheard, Destiny doesn't want to go back to school. I can't say I blame her. The poor thing is starting to show. I bet she gets teased."

"I'm sure that would be hard on her. Maybe her mom can have her homeschooled."

"I don't see how she could possibly take that on. She already has two jobs," Tara reminded me.

"True. Maybe you could homeschool her."

"Me?" Tara shrieked.

"Why not? You're supersmart and you always did well in school. Destiny can work here part-time and do her schoolwork in the office part-time while her mom's at work. It seems like a good way to keep track of her, and make sure she doesn't fall too far behind during her pregnancy."

I could see Tara was considering it. "Do you think Destiny would go for it?"

"You won't know until you ask."

Tara went to help a customer who had come in, so I decided to call Finn. It occurred to me that if Roxi had deposited the money Greg had given her into the bank, there had to be a paper trail.

Finn confirmed that he'd checked into Roxi's financial records and found an account with over fifty grand in it.

"Fifty grand? That makes no sense. Are you sure?"

"I'm sure. She opened the account with a five-thousand-dollar deposit about six weeks ago. There were a series of smaller deposits for a grand or two each, followed by a deposit for fifteen grand. Then she withdrew twenty grand. After that there were a bunch of small deposits as well as two large ones, one for ten grand and, most recently, one for thirty-five grand."

"Becky Wood told me Roxi sold Jimmy's boat. I'm not an expert on the going rates for boats, but thirty-five grand sounds about right. It was a large boat, though I heard the engine was on the way out. Ernie Wall gave Roxi five grand about six weeks ago, after she came to work with a black eye. I'm going to go out on a limb and guess that the five grand he gave her is what she used to open the account. I also know that Tony Sommers gave Roxi fifteen grand, and although Brianna just found out about it, it seems that fifteen grand most likely came from him. Stacy told me Jimmy was in debt to some thug for twenty grand, so I'm going to assume she used the twenty grand she withdrew to pay the guy off."

"Seems like a reasonable theory, which confirms a lot of what I've already discovered," Finn agreed.

"I spoke to Angie at the library today. She told me that Roxi was late for their church group a couple of weeks ago because she had to stop off at the bank and deposit some money a friend gave her. She thought his name was Greg. I recently heard that Greg Westlake told his mother that he was moving out of her basement and in with Roxi. At first I figured that rumor was just bragging on Greg's part because Roxi was way out of his league, but what if Greg gave Roxi a large amount of money and she rewarded him the way she seems to have been rewarding everyone else who gave her money?"

"With sex."

"Exactly. It seems it might be worth your time to have a chat with Greg," I said.

"I'll head over to his place now."

Chapter 9

My phone rang just as I was getting into my car to head back to town. It was Cody.

"Hey, what's up?"

"I'm down at the dock to see if anyone knows what Jimmy might have been in to before he died. I've already had two people tell me Danny hasn't shown up at his boat for two days."

"Two days? It rained yesterday, so I suppose it makes sense that he might have spent the day in town, but he had charters on Sunday, and I'm sure he would have gone home by now even if he didn't have any today. Are these people reliable?"

"The guy with the bald head and big gut who works in the marina office told me Danny didn't show up for his charters on Sunday. He knows because a representative from each group came into the office and asked if he had a way to contact Danny. He said he called Danny's cell and left a message."

I had to admit that sounded bad.

"And the other source?"

"That guy with the long hair who lives a couple of slips down from Danny."

"Caleb?"

"Yeah, that's him. He said he hadn't seen Danny since Saturday, and his boat hasn't left the slip since he came in from his last charter on Saturday."

"I'm coming over," I decided. "Where exactly are you?"

"Standing in front of Danny's boat. I took a look around and nothing looks disturbed, but there's no sign he's been here recently either."

"Okay, stay where you are. I'll be right there."

It wasn't like Danny to just disappear, and although he did tend to miss some messages regarding changes to his previously scheduled charters, it wasn't like him to flake out entirely. I remembered him telling me that he had charters all day Sunday when I'd spoken to him on Saturday. He'd seemed to be planning to meet those obligations, so why hadn't he? More importantly, where was he and why hadn't he called? We'd had rain the previous day, so I hadn't had the occasion to call him with last-minute reservations. When he hadn't shown up last evening, I'd assumed he was hanging out at the bar, as he often did. I was really worried.

I was tempted to call Tara to ask her if she'd seen or spoken to him, but I didn't want to send her into hysterics if she hadn't. I figured it was better to head to the marina to find out what I could before I sent my best friend into panic mode. Danny was a capable person who, I believed, could look out for himself, but given all the odd things that had been going on, I felt a lot less confident than I normally would.

When I arrived at the marina I found Cody and Max waiting for me on the deck of Danny's boat. It was a beautiful day, and even if Danny didn't have any tours scheduled I would think he'd be working on the boat. He had an old boat that required quite a lot of tender loving care, which meant that when he wasn't on the water he was usually working on it.

I looked around the marina. It was pretty deserted. A Tuesday during the off season didn't normally lend itself to a lot of tourist activity even if the weather cooperated.

"Do you know if Danny had any tours scheduled?" Cody asked me.

"Yeah, he has one in about an hour. He really should be here by now. And I know he had four charters on Sunday. Tara mentioned to me that the first charter of the day had canceled, which left three. I did see a notation next to the last one, indicating that they were going to call Danny that day to confirm because they had a potential conflict. That still left the middle two charters."

"Which must be the two the guy in the marina office mentioned to me."

"Gus."

"Yeah, Gus. He gave them Danny's cell number, but he never picked up."

"I'm surprised neither of the customers has called Coffee Cat Books to complain."

"Gus must have handled it."

"I say we hang out to see if either Danny or his customers show up for the charter scheduled for this afternoon," I said. "In the meantime, I'm going to walk over to have a chat with Caleb."

Caleb and Danny were friends. Caleb ran a fishing charter, and they both lived on their boats and both depended on the seasonal tourist dollar to survive. Chances were if Danny was up to anything Caleb would know about it.

"Hey, Caleb, you in there?" I called from the dock.

He poked his head out of the cabin. "Hey, Cait. What are you doing here? Did you bring me coffee?"

I shook my head. "Sorry. I wanted to ask about Danny. Cody told me that Gus said Danny missed his Sunday charters."

"Yeah. He didn't show up for the entire day."

"Do you have any idea where he might have gone?" I asked.

"Not a clue. We talked on Saturday. He told me he was having dinner with you and that he might stay at Maggie's due to the storm. He mentioned he had a busy day on Sunday and that he planned to take every charter he could while folks were still looking to go out. I never saw him come back on Sunday, but I had an early group, so he might have returned while I was gone. It really doesn't make sense that he'd flake out on his groups unless he had a really good reason."

"Yeah." I sighed. "The whole thing makes no sense."

"Guess you could ask Gus if he saw Danny on Sunday before the charters he missed. Gerrie was around as well."

Gerrie was a sixty-four-year-old widow who lived in the boat at the end of the dock closest to the wharf. She was a seasonal resident who left the island every

October and returned the following May. During the five months she was on site she liked to sit on her deck and people watch. If Danny had come home on Sunday morning she'd know about it.

Unfortunately, Gerrie wasn't at home, so I headed over to the marina office to chat with Gus, who was always around. He was an interesting sort of person, as salty and crusty as an old whaling captain, but as far as I knew, the closest he ever got to the sea was his office at the entrance to the marina. He'd once let it slip, after he'd had a few shots, that he didn't know how to swim and was terrified of the water.

"Hey, Gus," I greeted him.

"Young Hart."

"I came to ask if you saw Danny at all on Sunday."

"The kid missed his charters. Caused a huge hullabaloo that I had to deal with."

"I know. And thank you for taking care of things. I was wondering if you saw him before that, though. He spent the night at Maggie's, but I know he planned to return to his boat once he left there in the morning."

"Didn't see him."

"And you haven't seen him since Saturday?" I confirmed.

"Nope. If he's going to miss any more charters someone needs to call his customers to give them a heads-up. I don't want to have to deal with the fuss I did on Sunday again."

"I will. He has a reservation today, but I'll stay to deal with it if he doesn't show up. If you see or hear from him will you please call me, or ask him to call me? I'm really starting to worry about him."

"I'm sure the boy is fine. Probably just tied one on and forgot all about his customers. If I do hear from him, I'll call you."

I thanked Gus and returned to Danny's boat to wait. Cody was on his phone, so I sat down on the edge of the deck and cuddled with Max, who was thrilled to have me around in the middle of the day. I looked out at the water and wondered if I should call Finn. Danny would kill me if I got him involved and it turned out he'd simply been shacking up with some chick he'd met somewhere along the way. Danny did have a tendency to throw responsibility aside when it came to his infatuations with the women who seemed to fade in and out of his life.

Cody hung up and walked over to join me. He sat down next to me.

"I don't suppose that was Danny?" I asked hopefully.

"Finn."

"What did he want?"

"He got a lead that Garrett Goldman had been seen hanging around with the same guy Jimmy had been right before his death, so he went out to his place to talk to him. When he got there he found Garrett unconscious in his living room. He's alive, but just barely. They're airlifting him to the hospital in Seattle."

Garrett Goldman was a crusty old fisherman who owned a large lot on the north shore of Madrona Island. His land had its own dock, which gave him easy access to the open sea. Jimmy and Garrett had been friends, so it sort of made sense that they might have been involved in the same business deal.

"Oh, no. Poor Garrett. Did Finn have any idea what happened?"

"Only that he had been beaten up. I doubt we'll know more until Garrett regains consciousness. Finn is going to have a look around his place, but as of a few minutes ago, he hadn't picked up anything new." Cody pointed to a group of Asian men who were getting out of a van. "It looks like Danny's group is here."

"I'll go talk to them," I offered. "Call Finn back to tell him about Danny. If he's mixed up in whatever the others were, he could be in real danger."

Chapter 10

Once I'd broken the news to Danny's group that there wasn't going to be a tour that afternoon, I decided I'd better fill Tara in on what was going on. I knew she'd be upset, but I also knew she'd eventually find out and be even madder that I hadn't kept her in the loop. We decided to meet with Finn to come up with a strategy to track Danny down, so we closed Coffee Cat Books and headed out to my cabin.

"I checked Danny's phone records," Finn informed us once Cody, Tara, Finn, and I had gathered around my kitchen table. Destiny was tired, so she'd headed up to my bedroom to take a nap with Beatrice, who still had yet to make her move.

"The last call to his cell that was answered was on Sunday morning at six a.m. It lasted less than a minute, and it looks as if his phone was turned off after he completed that call."

"Who did he speak to?" I asked.

"Melanie Hannigan."

Melanie was a waitress at O'Malley's who Danny dated occasionally.

"Did you talk to her?" I asked.

Finn nodded. She said she was lonely and wanted some company, so she called Danny, and he turned her down. It was obvious she was lying, but I could tell she was scared."

"Can't you force her to talk?" I asked.

"How am I supposed to do that?"

"Torture," I suggested.

Finn raised one eyebrow.

"If Danny is mixed up in whatever got Jimmy killed and Garrett beat up, maybe we should start to look for a link between the three," Tara said.

I'd really expected Tara to be having a major meltdown, but she actually seemed to be keeping it together better than I was. Even when we were kids, Tara had been good in a crisis. One minute after it had passed and things were okay, she'd have a complete meltdown, but during the actual event she'd always been a real trooper.

"I can think of two links between Jimmy, Garrett, and Danny," I began. "They all owned boats and they all hung out at O'Malley's. Prior to her death, Roxi was also spending a lot of time at the bar. It seems like O'Malley's is the key. We need to get Melanie to talk."

"Let me try," Cody offered.

I frowned. "Why you? I'm Danny's sister. Maybe I can play on her emotions."

"Melanie isn't the type to care about the fact that Danny's little sister is upset," Cody pointed out. "She's been hitting on me ever since I returned to the island. I think I can use that to get her to talk."

"Cody's right. He has the best shot," Finn agreed.

Cody slid off the bar stool he was sitting on and headed toward the door. "I'll call you as soon as I know anything."

And with that he was gone.

"So what about us?" Tara asked Finn. "How can Cait and I help?"

"If I suggested that you wait here until Cody and I get back to you, I don't suppose you'd comply?"

"I don't suppose we would," I answered.

"Look, whoever is behind all this is dangerous. I really do think you should let me take care of it."

I looked at Finn. "What exactly is your plan?"

"You correctly stated that the links between all three men were O'Malley's and the fact that they owned boats. Cody is talking to Melanie, so I'm going to pay a visit to all three boats to take another look around. Maybe I'll find something that might provide a clue as to what might be going on. I need the two of you to stay here."

I glanced at Tara but didn't answer.

"Besides, you have a pregnant teenager to look after," Finn added.

"Very well. We'll wait here for now. But you need to promise to check in with us within the next hour."

"Okay," Finn reluctantly agreed. "I'll check in."

"By the way," I stopped Finn as he got up to leave, "were you able to speak to Greg?"

"I was. He confirmed that he'd been giving Roxi money: one large sum of ten grand, as well as several smaller amounts, as he was able to dig up the money. He's convinced he and Roxi had a serious relationship, and that she wanted him to move in with her. I asked him if he knew she'd sold her boat and planned to leave the island, and he seemed genuinely distressed. I think he really thought they were going to live happily ever after, but it looks like she was just scamming him for the money."

"It sounds like Roxi might have cracked under the pressure. The Roxi I knew before Jimmy's death wouldn't have acted the way she apparently did toward the end."

"If you want my opinion, I think in the beginning she did owe this thug a bunch of money. She shared her sob story with a few people like Ernie and Tony and then realized how easy it was to get people to give her money. I think she became addicted to the rush involved with milking good people out of their hard-earned cash, so she kept doing it even after she'd paid off the debt."

"So you don't think the hit man killed her?"

"Honestly, I don't. The evidence indicates that Roxi had paid off Jimmy's debt. At this point, I'm betting on a jealous wife."

Finn called twenty minutes later to say that Garrett's boat was no longer tied to the dock. He hadn't looked for it earlier that day because he'd found Garrett half dead in his living room. It was Finn's opinion that whoever had beaten Garrett up most likely took the boat. Finn had called the coast guard and provided a description of the boat. Then he'd headed over to Danny's boat to see what he could find there.

I for one was tired of waiting around for Finn or Cody to find Danny, so I'd decided to take matters into my own hands and head to O'Malley's while Tara stayed with Destiny. I was just about to pull onto the highway from the peninsula road when Cody drove up from the opposite direction. He indicated he had news, so I turned around and followed him back to the cabin.

"Did Melanie have anything to say?" I asked.

"Actually, she did." Cody poured himself a glass of water. "She admitted that she'd called Danny on Sunday morning and told him that she was in trouble. She'd asked him to meet her at the bar, although she was safe at home, nowhere near the bar."

I frowned. "Why?"

"She said a man she knows only as Hawk came by her place and threatened to kill her if she didn't do what he asked. He told her he wanted to talk to Danny, so she called him, as she was ordered to do."

"Danny could be in real danger," Tara screeched. "I can't believe she set him up like that."

"Melanie is scared of this Hawk character, and it seems she has good reason to be. She thinks he's behind Jimmy's death."

"Okay, let's back up a bit," I said. "Who is this Hawk and why would he kill Jimmy?"

Cody slid onto a bar stool across from where I was standing. "Melanie doesn't have all the facts. What she does know is that Jimmy showed up at the bar with a man he introduced as Hawk about a month before he died. At first the pair seemed to be friends, and based on the way they sequestered themselves in a corner booth to chat, she believes they were into something together. A few days after Jimmy was killed in the auto accident, Melanie saw Hawk at the bar with Garrett. She said the two men had been meeting every couple of weeks there since then."

"What about Danny?" I asked.

"Melanie says no. She swears that whatever was going on seemed to be between Jimmy and Hawk, and then Garrett and Hawk."

"So what were they up to?" Tara asked.

"She swears she had no idea. She did say that a few days before Jimmy was killed she noticed there was a tension between him and Hawk. She saw them arguing in the parking lot two nights before Jimmy's accident, although she was too far away to hear what the fight was about. When Jimmy died she initially thought this Hawk guy had killed him, but then Finn and everyone else said his death was an accident, so she kept her mouth shut."

"When was the last time she saw Hawk?" I asked.

"When he showed up in her bedroom early on Sunday morning."

"He was in her bedroom?" Tara gasped.

"Melanie told me she was sound asleep but was awakened by someone putting a hand over her mouth. She opened her eyes and saw someone standing over her. Once her eyes adjusted to the darkness she realized it was Hawk. He had a gun and threatened to kill her unless she called Danny and told him to meet her at the bar. She panicked and did as he asked. She regretted what she'd done and had been hiding out, waiting for Danny to resurface ever since."

"That was Sunday. This is Tuesday. She could have called Finn or me or *someone* once Hawk left her place," I insisted.

"I agree. She's pretty traumatized. I don't think she knew what to do."

"Did Melanie know why this Hawk wanted to talk to Danny?" Tara asked.

"She said she didn't."

"Finn called to say Garrett's boat is gone. What if this Hawk needed a boat for some reason and needed someone who knew how to pilot a boat the size of Garrett's?" Tara asked. "Maybe he argued with Garrett and the outcome was that Garrett was beaten and left for dead, so Hawk decided to find someone else in the area who would be able to pilot Garrett's boat. Danny hangs out at O'Malley's, so Hawk would most likely know who he was. He'd most likely know that he knows his way around boats, so he kidnapped him."

"Yeah, but Danny went missing on Sunday. Today is Tuesday," I said again. "Where has he been for three days?"

No one answered.

"I'm really worried about Danny. I don't think I can just sit here and wait for whatever's going to happen to happen," I insisted.

"What do you want to do?" Cody asked.

"I don't know. Take Danny's boat and look for Garrett's boat?"

"Why don't we see if O'Malley knows anything?" Cody suggested. "Just because Melanie didn't know what Jimmy, Garrett, and Hawk were up to doesn't mean O'Malley doesn't."

Cody and I headed to O'Malley's while Tara stayed behind with Destiny.

It took my eyes a minute to adjust from the bright sunshine after I walked into the dark bar. The bar was almost always full during its operating hours, but at this time of day the place was completely deserted. O'Malley's was old-fashioned, with dark wood, a rustic atmosphere, and dart boards on the wall. Unlike many of the bars I'd frequented in Seattle, it was completely devoid of plants, fish, or artsy décor. While O'Malley's carried a good selection of liquor, most customers were there for a beer or a shot.

"O'Malley, are you here?" I called as I entered the deserted bar.

"Hang on, I'm in the back," a voice responded.

Cody and I sat down on adjacent bar stools, waiting for the bar owner to appear. The rustic place held a lot of good memories for me. I'd come here on my twenty-first birthday; most islanders did. It was sort of a local rite of passage. I'd had my first shot and, as far as my mother needed to know, my first beer. I'd celebrated other milestones in the large booth in the corner, which was a perfect place to meet up with friends.

"Hey, Cait; Cody. What's up?"

"We wanted to chat with you about the recent rash of insanity that's hit the island if you have a minute," Cody began.

"I guess I could take a break." O'Malley held up a bottle of good Irish whiskey. "Shot?"

"No thanks," Cody and I both answered.

O'Malley poured a shot for himself and leaned on the bar across from us. "So what's on your mind?"

"We've learned that both Jimmy and Garrett were meeting with a man in the bar that so far I've only heard referred to as Hawk," I began.

O'Malley nodded. "I know the guy you're talking about."

"Do you know anything about him? How long he's been on the island? Where he came from?" I asked.

"I'd never seen him before he showed up maybe a month before Jimmy's accident. I don't know where he's from originally, but he's tall and thin, with dark hair and a beard."

"Do you have any idea what he and Jimmy and Garrett might have been up to?"

"No, not really. They always kept their voices low, and it does get noisy in here.

If I had to guess I'd say smuggling was at the heart of their relationship."

"Smuggling? Smuggling what?"

O'Malley shrugged. "Drugs, artifacts, jewels, people. Who knows? Seemed like this Hawk character was more interested in the boats Jimmy and Garrett could provide than the men themselves."

That actually made sense. International water wasn't all that far away, and once you smuggled whatever it was you were bringing onto the island, it would be easy to transport it to the mainland via the ferry or even a private boat. From there you could take it anywhere and never have to go through customs or border patrol.

"Danny is missing," I blurted out. I really hadn't planned to share this piece of information with O'Malley; I wasn't 100 percent sure he wasn't somehow involved in this whole thing, but I found myself saying it anyway.

"Missing? Since when?" O'Malley looked surprised, so perhaps he really didn't know what was going on.

Cody filled him in on what Melanie had told him.

"Please, if you can think of anything," I begged. "If Hawk has Danny we need to figure out what he's up to."

"I'm sorry, but I really have no idea why he'd want Danny or where he might have taken him."

Cody and I returned to the cabin. Tara had made a casserole and Destiny was helping her prepare a dessert. There was no way I was going to be able to eat, but I supposed cooking gave Tara and Destiny something to do.

"Any news?" Tara asked anxiously.

"Not yet."

"The coast guard has helicopters combing the area," Cody assured me. "I'm sure it's only a matter of time before they find Garrett's boat."

"And if Danny isn't on it?" I wondered.

"Then we'll figure out what to do next." Cody put his arm around me.

"I wonder if I should tell Aunt Maggie what's going on. And my mom. God, my mom is going to freak."

"It's only been a couple of hours since Finn contacted the coast guard. Let's wait to hear back. If they don't find the boat right away I'll go with you to tell Maggie and your mom. If they do find him right away and he's unharmed, we can save both women some worry by waiting."

"Yeah, you have a good point. We'll wait a couple of hours. But if they don't find him..."

"Then we'll tell them what's going on," Cody promised.

I began to pace around the cabin. There was no way I was going to be able to sit still until Danny was found. I knew the coast guard was trained to do exactly what they were doing at that moment. Now I just had to trust that they'd find Danny and he was okay.

"Maybe Garrett knows something," I commented. "Do we know if he's regained consciousness?"

"It's been several hours since he was transported to Seattle. I'll see if I can get an update," Cody volunteered.

I looked out the window at the sea just beyond my cabin while Cody called Finn. I knew if Hawk had been heading for open water Danny could be miles away by now, yet still I willed Garrett's boat to magically appear from beyond the horizon. If Danny had been kidnapped on Sunday that meant he had been out at sea on Monday during the storm. I didn't want to imagine all the horrible things that could have happened to him.

"He's still unconscious," Cody informed me after he hung up with Finn. "The good news is that they've stabilized him and they think he's going to make a full recovery. He's been sedated, but Finn assured me that he'll make the trip to Seattle to talk to him the minute he wakes up."

"And Danny?"

"No news yet. But they aren't giving up. They'll search until dark, and if they still haven't found him they'll resume the search tomorrow. Danny is smart. He's resourceful. I'm sure he's fine."

"He's with a madman who's probably killed at least one other person. You can't know he'll be fine," I cried.

Cody wrapped his arms around me and pulled me toward his chest, hugging me in an offer of support. I knew I shouldn't be snapping at him. He was only trying to help. But snapping was the only thing I could think of to do.

Cody's phone rang. I pulled back slightly and held my breath while he looked at the caller ID. "It's Finn."

It felt like my heart stopped beating as I waited, suspended in time, to hear whether they'd found Danny and if he was still alive. Tara crossed the room and took my hand in hers.

"The coast guard found Danny," Cody informed us. "He's fine."

I let out the breath I'd been holding and hugged Tara. Tears streamed down both our faces. Cody spoke to Finn for a few minutes and then hung up. He smiled as he turned toward us.

"Where did they find him?" I asked.

"I don't know specifically," Cody said. "What I do know is that he's been floating around in Garrett's boat for several days. The vessel as well as its communication system had been disabled. They're bringing him in now."

"And he's not hurt?"

"The coast guard told Finn that Danny was hungry and dehydrated but otherwise unharmed."

"Does Finn know what happened?"

"He spoke to Danny for just a moment over the radio and he doesn't have all the details, but he did say Danny confirmed that Melanie had called him in a panic before the sun had even come up on Sunday morning. She'd told him that she was in trouble and asked him to meet her at O'Malley's. He went, but when he got there she was nowhere to be found. He'd just gotten back into his car to leave when a man with a gun slid into his passenger seat and told him to drive out to Garrett's. Naturally, he complied. When they got there he was escorted to Garrett's boat.

Hawk demanded that he take it out to open water, where they met up with a cruise ship from South America that was heading to Alaska. Hawk disabled Garrett's boat and then boarded the cruise ship. Danny didn't have any way to navigate, so he's just been drifting around, waiting to be rescued."

"Poor Danny. Did he know why Hawk wanted to meet up with the ship?"

"Finn didn't say. I guess we can ask Danny when he gets here. Finn said the coast guard planned to drop him off on the island within the hour, and he's going to meet them. He said he'd call back once he picks Danny up."

It turned out Danny had no idea why Hawk wanted to meet up with the cruise ship. After he'd kidnapped him, he brought Danny to Garrett's boat and gave him the coordinates he wanted him to head toward. Danny got the impression Hawk didn't know how to navigate the boat on his own. When I asked why he had Danny take Garrett's boat rather than his own, Danny said he probably realized Garrett's boat was docked in a private location close to open water, whereas they'd have to navigate through the harbor in order to get to Danny's. Anyone could have seen them and he would have had ample opportunity to escape.

Danny had had very little food and water for days, so he was both hungry and dehydrated, but otherwise he seemed fine. Once we'd fed him fatigue set in, so he'd headed to Maggie's to catch up on his sleep.

The coast guard planned to catch up with the cruise ship to see if they could track down Hawk. Finn didn't think he'd still be with the ship; that would have made him too easy to find. If he hadn't been planning to disappear from the ship he most likely would have killed Danny to leave behind no witnesses who would know he'd boarded the ship in the first place.

Once Danny had headed over to Maggie's, Cody and Tara went home. I settled Destiny on the sofa and tried to go to sleep myself, but my mind simply wouldn't shut down. I decided to head downstairs and heat some milk. My mom used to make me warm milk when I couldn't sleep when I was a kid. Most times it still did the trick.

I tried to tiptoe quietly down to the kitchen, but I guess I wasn't quiet enough.

"Is something wrong?" Destiny sat up and looked at me.

"I'm sorry. I didn't mean to wake you. I just came down for a glass of milk."

"Actually, I'm kind of hungry. Do you mind if I join you?"

"Not at all. Feel free to eat or drink whatever you want while you're here. Can I make you something?"

"Maybe just some toast and a glass of milk. My stomach usually isn't fond of anything heavy at night." Destiny rubbed her growing belly.

I turned on the small light over the counter area, which provided just enough illumination for us to see what we were doing. I popped a couple of slices of bread in the toaster and poured a tall glass of milk. Beatrice had already had her dinner, but I felt guilty that I'd initiated this whole middle-of-the-night pig-out, so I gave her and Max a small scoop of food.

"I don't think Beatrice is happy with the food you gave her." Destiny laughed as the silly cat swatted at the bowl, eventually tipping it over and spilling the contents all over the floor.

"If you didn't want me to fill your bowl why are you sitting in front if it?" I groaned.

"I think maybe your cat is defective," Destiny said. "Tara told me how some of the other cats Tansy has sent you have helped you out with mysteries in the past, but this one seems to be a dud."

"She certainly hasn't done anything to help us so far. It's only been a few days; maybe it just isn't time for her to show us whatever it is she's here for yet."

Destiny pressed her hands into her back.

"Backache?" I asked.

"Yeah. They seem to be getting worse the bigger I become."

"You know I love having you here, but I can't help but wonder if you'll ever get a good night's sleep on my lumpy old sofa."

"I'm not going home."

"I know. I wasn't suggesting that. I was just wondering if maybe we should talk to Tara about you staying with her. She has an extra bedroom with a real bed."

Destiny shrugged. "If she wants me that would be okay. If not, the sofa is fine."

"I'm sure you must be getting to the stage in your pregnancy where you're uncomfortable in more ways than one."

"All the time." Destiny rubbed her belly with one hand.

"I guess the good news is that you don't have too much longer to wait." Destiny had told me she was six months along.

"Yeah." A look of longing came over the girl's face.

"Have you decided what you're going to do after the baby's born?"

Destiny bit her lip. It looked like she was going to cry. *Good going, Cait.*

"No," Destiny whispered quietly. "Everyone thinks I should give it up for adoption, but I don't know if I can. When I first found out I was pregnant I totally freaked out and wanted to rip it from my body. And then when Ricky said he was breakin' up with me because he was too young to be a father, I thought I would die. But now... I don't know. Now that I can feel it movin' around it seems real to me. I know I'm young and I know my mom can't afford to feed another mouth, but it's mine and I just don't see how I can give it to a stranger."

I put my arm around Destiny. "You have time to figure out what you want to do. Whatever you decide, I want you to know I'll be here for you."

Destiny put her arms around my neck and began to sob. I couldn't imagine how hard it would be to be having a child when you were still a child yourself. I had to agree with popular opinion that the wisest choice would be for her to give her baby up for adoption, but if I was the one with

the unplanned pregnancy, I'm not sure I could give my baby away either.

Chapter 11

Friday, September 25

Three days had passed since we found Danny, and he was pretty much fully recovered. He even planned to accept charters for the weekend. Beatrice continued with her pattern of sleeping for half the day and ignoring me the other half. Next time I'm going to ask Tansy to quality check the cats she sends me. I thought about asking for an exchange on this one, but Tansy hadn't returned from her retreat yet and Bella claimed not to know when she'd be back.

Tara, Destiny, and I were planning to help my mom with the kiddie carnival at the St. Patrick's dinner that evening. Destiny had decided to stay with Tara, who was thrilled to have the company. Destiny is very helpful in the bookstore, and the two of them are getting along like peas in a pod. I hope we've found a temporary solution to the conflict between Destiny and her mother. I knew the girl has a tough road ahead and a lot of really difficult decisions to make, but she seemed to have dropped her plan to leave the island. She also seemed to be getting along a lot better with her mother now that she wasn't trying to force her to go to school.

"Did the bookmarks we ordered ever arrive?" I asked Tara as I sorted through the boxes that had come over on the morning ferry.

"Not yet. I guess I should call the supplier to see what the delay is all about. We still have some in the back room from the last shipment if you need to restock."

"We're okay for now; I was just straightening things up and it occurred to me to ask. We're getting low on the large mugs and the Coffee Cat Books pot holders. We should have Destiny go through all the inventory when she gets back. I bet there are other items we might want to reorder while we're at it."

"That'd be a good job for her today," Tara agreed as she picked up one of the boxes and slit open the top.

"She still at the high school?"

"Yeah. I expect her back any time," Tara said as she began to check the contents of the box against the packing slip.

Destiny and her mom had been required to meet with the principal at the school to work out a homeschool program that would be counted as regular high school credit because Destiny still hoped to return to the school for her senior year. While she lived with Tara and worked at Coffee Cat Books, Sister Mary, who had a teaching degree because the church where she was prior to St. Patrick's had a school, would oversee Destiny's curriculum.

"I heard Garrett has regained consciousness," Tara commented as we worked side by side to sort through the delivery and restock the shelves.

"I spoke to Finn earlier, and he said it happened yesterday morning," I confirmed. "He went to talk to him in the afternoon. I don't know if I would consider the case to be closed, but Garrett did fill in a few of the blanks."

"So catch me up." Tara stopped what she was doing and looked at me.

"Apparently, after Jimmy died, Hawk approached him about joining him in a moneymaking operation that dealt with moving cargo between a cruise ship that made regular trips between South America and Alaska and a warehouse in Seattle."

Tara frowned. "I don't get it. Why would they want to move cargo off the cruise ship when they could just wait until they docked in Alaska?"

"Garrett believes the cargo was illegal and would never have made it through customs. He said Hawk hired him to meet up with the cruise ship out in the open sea. He was given a date and a preset time during each of the ship's voyages. Once he'd tied up with the cruise ship, he was given crates by a crew member he knew only as Pablo. He was told to bring the crates back to the island via his own vessel and then transport them via his vehicle and the ferry to a warehouse just outside Seattle. Once he delivered the crates to the warehouse, he was to return to the ferry terminal in Anacortes, where he was given a locked black duffel bag. He was instructed to deliver the bag to Hawk and wait for instructions concerning the next pickup. He was told that five thousand dollars would be deposited into an offshore account in his name for every delivery he completed."

"Wait; so if he met up with the ship, the captain must have been in on whatever was going on," Tara realized.

"It would seem so. Garrett told Finn that he would be given a set of coordinates along with a specific time. When he arrived the ship would be there and Pablo would meet him in one of the shuttle boats, along with a crate or crates that he was to transport that day. He said once the cargo was on his vessel, Pablo would return to the cruise ship and it would continue on its way."

"It seems like the passengers would wonder what was going on."

"Garrett said he always met the ship after dark. If anyone did question what was going on, I'm sure the captain had some sort of a canned response. Chances were most of the passengers were inside dining or enjoying the casino or an evening show. Should I put out these new book bags?"

"No, let's sell the ones we have on display first," Tara answered. "So what was in the cartons?"

"Garrett didn't know. He was never told what was in them or where their eventual destination was. I know that after Garrett told Seattle law enforcement about the warehouse it was searched, but it was empty at that point."

"So what about whoever gave Garrett the duffel bag at the ferry? Can they track that person down?"

"Finn said Garrett gave a description of the man who always delivered the duffel bag, but so far they haven't been able to identify him," I told her.

Tara picked up the box she had been unpacking and carried it over to the door leading out onto the wharf. We'd started a pile, which we planned to take out to the Dumpster once we were finished restocking the shelves.

"Okay, so how did Jimmy end up owing Hawk twenty grand?" Tara asked as she picked up a new box and slit open the top.

"Garrett told Finn that when he heard about the trouble Roxi was having with Hawk, he asked him about it. Hawk said Jimmy had twenty grand he was supposed to deliver to Hawk, but he died in the accident before he did. Roxi insisted she didn't have the money or know where it was, but Hawk didn't believe her."

"So it looks like our theory that Hawk killed Jimmy was wrong."

"It looks that way," I confirmed. "That is, if both Hawk and Garrett are telling the truth. Jimmy's accident occurred on his way back from the ferry after delivering one of the crates. It's Finn's new theory that Jimmy had the duffel bag with him, and that the bag contained the twenty grand. Finn believes someone knew about the money, caused the accident, and then stole the duffel bag."

"So there's a second bad guy?" Tara groaned.

"If Finn's theory is correct. I wonder if we should make room in the window for these new releases."

"Yeah, go ahead and move some of the books that have been out the longest to the rack near the checkstand. I think I'd like to redo the entire display after this weekend. It's getting to be time to think about Halloween."

"My favorite holiday." I grinned. "Hopefully we'll be murder free and can relax and have some fun."

"Tell me about it," Tara agreed. "We've certainly had our share of murders lately."

"It's pretty odd the way the bodies keep showing up."

"This entire investigation began with us wanting to find out what happened to Roxi," Tara pointed out. "Do we think Hawk killed Roxi for some reason?"

"Garrett doesn't think so. Roxi paid Hawk what Jimmy owed. He seemed to think Hawk considered them square. My money is still on a jealous wife."

"Okay, then, which one? We know Brianna Sommers was furious when she found out about Tony and Roxi, but it seems like that was after Roxi was already dead. Becky Wood told you that she wanted to kill Roxi for messing around with Trace, but she also said she felt less threatened once she found out she had sold her boat and was planning to leave."

"All of that is true."

"I heard Roxi was seen with Griff Poolman," Tara offered.

I remembered hearing that as well. "Maybe someone should have a chat with Jean," I said, referring to Griff's wife.

"I'll talk to her," Tara volunteered. "We took that cooking class at the community center together last summer, so we sort of know each other."

"You know who else we might want to talk to? Pink Headband."

"Come again?"

"The woman who always wears the pink headband in our exercise class. I can't remember her name."

"Viveca," Tara supplied.

"Right, Viveca. We were discussing Bitzy and her cheating husband on Tuesday and Viveca seemed to get really upset about the fact that Bitzy's husband had cheated on her. She said she knew what it felt like to have the person you loved betray you. I have no idea if her husband knew Roxi, but it couldn't hurt to talk to her."

"Viveca mentioned she would be attending the ball tomorrow night," Tara said. "Maybe we can track her down and talk to her there."

"She might be at the dinner at St. Pat's tonight as well. I think a couple of her kids attend the group on Tuesdays."

"You know, the killer could be one of the men," Tara pointed out. "Roxi scammed them all. I could see how some lovesick fool would feel betrayed when he found out Roxi had conned money out of multiple men and didn't really seem to care about any of them."

"I don't know." I frowned. "It seems like the guys Roxi conned are all worldly enough to shake it off. I mean, most of the men are married. I bet their main concern would be to keep their wives from finding out what they'd done."

"What about Gary?" Tara asked. "He was single and a lot more naive than the others. You don't think..."

"No," I answered. "Finn told me Gary was seriously distraught when he found out Roxi was planning to leave the island. Finn seemed convinced he had no idea she was juggling a bunch of different guys. I know it seems like he must have known because *everyone* else did, but I think he was just a nerdy guy in love, probably for the first time, who chose to see only what he wanted to see."

"That's really kind of sad. I guess now that Roxi is gone he's going to be stuck living with his mother for who knows how long."

"Maybe and maybe not. Now that he's experienced love he might go looking for it again rather than being content to spend all his free time with his mom," I predicted.

"On the other hand, if he's too heartbroken he may have decided love isn't worth the risk."

"Been there." I laughed.

"Did you ever talk to Cody about the ball?"

"Actually, we did talk about it, and we're going together. With everything that's been going on, I haven't had any time to work on my costume, so I may show up in my bathrobe, though."

Tara giggled. "That could work. As long as you wear a mask of course."

"Of course. Did you ever decide whether to go with Carl?"

"I'd decided to go alone and just help out with the food, but Danny called me last night and asked if I wanted to go with him."

"Danny asked you out on a date?"

"I don't think so. I'm pretty sure he was asking me to go with him as a friend. But it still sounded a lot better than going alone, so I told him I would. Maybe if you're going with Cody the four of us can go together. It might help to ease any weirdness that might creep in."

"That sounds like fun." I smiled. "Cody and I are really just going as friends as well, so it will be nice to have you and Danny around. I'll ask Cody to talk to Danny about it. They can decide between them who wants to drive."

Chapter 12

Every year the Harvest Festival on Madrona Island kicks off with a celebration at St. Patrick's Catholic Church. Not only is there a huge community dinner but there are games and activities set up for the youth of our island as well. This year Tara, Cody, Destiny, and I all showed up early to help set up the kiddie carnival. One of the things I love the most about community events such as this one is the energy that's created when friends and neighbors come together to celebrate something that's important to all of us.

Living on a small island is a lot like being part of a large family. The isolated nature of our existence creates an intimacy that you might not normally find even in a small town. Although the ferry has certainly opened up the world for us, during the long winter months, when the days are short and few mainlanders make the trip west, the few thousand citizens living on the island depend on one another exclusively for both entertainment and support.

"Tell me again why we didn't rent a helium machine?" Cody asked as he tied the knot on the hundredth balloon he'd blown up for the dart toss.

"No one thought to reserve one. By the time the oversight was discovered it was way too late to bring one over from the mainland, so we're stuck doing it the old-fashioned way."

"Maybe I'll buy a helium machine and donate it to the church," Cody offered. "That way I won't have to worry about a repeat blowathon next year. Are you sure three darts for a dollar isn't too cheap? I'm afraid if we make the game too desirable I'll be blowing these darn things up all night."

"Hey, you offered to help," I reminded him. "Don't worry; most of the kids who play this have pretty awful aim. As long as the adults don't decide to join in, we should be fine."

I glanced around the room. It did look like we had more than our share of teens geared up to play the games this year. While the carnival was open to anyone, most of the time the island's teenagers congregated outside to hang, while only the younger kids met up with friends indoors to eat junk food and play games.

"Maybe we can recruit some reinforcements to help us blow up balloons once everyone else gets here," Cody said.

"We can even make it a game. Whoever blows up the most balloons in five minutes wins a prize."

"That's actually a really good idea. I knew there was a reason I requested we be teamed up tonight."

Cody winked and smiled at me. "Are my good ideas the only reason you wanted to pair up with me?"

I shot a yet-to-be inflated balloon at him. "Get your mind out of the gutter. We're in a church."

"Actually, we're in a church auditorium."

I rolled my eyes. "Did you call Danny about tomorrow night?"

"I did, and we're all set to sweep you girls off your feet."

"Oh, brother. You really need to stop watching all those soap operas with Mr. Parsons. You're starting to get overly sappy."

"You know I've always been sappy."

That was surprisingly true. Cody was famous for displaying a very interesting combination of traits including fearlessness, strength, and intelligence, as well as sensitivity, loyalty, and compassion. And yes, he'd even been known to tear up during a sad movie.

"Did they know you were such a girl when they accepted you into the Seals?" I teased.

"Absolutely." Cody winked again.

I laughed and kissed his cheek. There was something about this friend of mine that seemed to make me very happy. When Cody first returned to the island I wasn't sure I wanted him invading my space. Now I didn't know how I'd ever be happy without him.

"There's Pink Headband." I nodded to a woman who was standing in line for the fishing game with two adorable little girls. "I'm going to go talk to her. I'll be right back."

"Hurry. We still have a ton of balloons to blow up before we can open and the natives are getting restless."

"I'll be back in a jiff."

A jiff might have been an overstatement. It took me longer than that to make my way across the crowded room. Still, she was one of the only people still on the suspect list I'd made up to deal with Roxi's murder investigation, and I wanted to either confirm or eliminate my suspicions.

"Are these your daughters?" I asked the woman.

"They are. Lisa and Lori."

"They're adorable. And all that black hair. It's really beautiful." I glanced at Pink Headband's blond hair. "I bet your husband must have black hair; the girls didn't seem to get it from you."

"Actually, he has blond hair as well. The girls are adopted."

Good going, Cait.

"I'm sorry. I didn't realize."

Pink Headband shrugged. "That's okay. A lot of people make the same mistake. Even when Jason and I are together."

"I don't believe I've met your husband. Is he here tonight?"

"No. He's in Afghanistan. He's in the middle of his tour, so it will be a while until he's home again. The girls really miss him."

"I guess you must miss him as well."

Pink Headband shrugged. "I guess. I do miss having a man around to fix the plumbing and take out the garbage, but Jason and I were having problems before he left. I think this time away will be good for us. He's a good guy, but he sometimes makes dumb decisions."

"Yeah, I know a few guys like that."

If Jason was overseas he couldn't have been messing around with Roxi. Still, I did get the vibe that the trouble Pink Headband might have been having with her husband was woman-related. I supposed it was possible Jason could have been messing around with Roxi before he left, but somehow I doubted it.

"I guess I should get back to help Cody blow up balloons."

"Cody West is here? I hadn't seen him."

"He's over at the dart toss."

Pink Headband smiled. "Wonderful. I wanted to have a chance to catch up with him. I'd heard he was on the island, but so far we haven't run into each other."

"You know Cody from before he left for the Navy?" I asked. "I didn't know you'd lived here that long."

"I haven't. My cousin June lived on the island about twelve years ago. I met Cody at a party on the beach when I was visiting one summer. We really hit it off. I was thrilled to hear he'd moved back to Madrona. Do you know if he's seeing anyone? I've always wondered what it would be like to hook up with a man who looks like him."

I frowned. I looked at Pink Headband's two daughters, who were listening to our conversation. Was the woman nuts? If you're hoping to cheat on your husband while he's overseas fighting for our country, the least you could do is to refrain from talking about it in front of your own kids.

"I do think Cody is seeing someone," I answered.

Pink Headband looked disappointed. "Is it serious?"

"Serious enough. I really need to go. I'll see you in class on Tuesday."

I started back across the room with a scowl on my face. Some people really had a lot of nerve. I didn't understand a world where cheating on the man you'd committed to love for life was something to be taken so casually.

"Someone steal your puppy?" Tara asked when our paths crossed.

"Puppy?"

"The look on your face was so intense and so angry, all I could come up with was that someone had stolen your puppy."

"I just ran into Pink Headband," I explained. "Do you know what she had the nerve to say?"

I restated the conversation I'd just had with her to Tara.

"She really said that in front of her daughters?"

"She really did. The woman has no sense of morality, but I don't think she killed Roxi. Although ..." I hesitated. "She did make a statement about knowing what it was like to be betrayed by someone you thought loved you. Maybe there's more to her relationship with her husband than meets the eye. Did you ever talk to Jean Poolman?"

Tara nodded. "I don't think she did it. She was upset about the way Roxi was coming on to Griff, but she didn't seem upset enough to kill her. I think we need to keep looking."

"Yeah, I had the same thought myself. Do you know who that kid is who Destiny is talking to?" I asked.

Tara looked across the room. "No; why?"

"I haven't seen her hanging out with any kids her age since she's been with us. She did mention she had a friend named Jake who she described as her *only* friend. I don't want to interrupt their conversation, but if that's Jake, I want to talk to him about Roxi."

"Why would you want to talk to a high school kid about Roxi? I know she'd been dating around, but I don't think even she would date a teenager."

"I don't think he dated her. Destiny mentioned that he lived next door to her. I thought he might have seen or heard something."

I watched as Destiny laughed at something the boy said to her. I was actually kind of surprised she'd wanted to come. She's been sensitive to the other kids' teasing about her impending motherhood. It seemed spending time with Tara had been good for her. I felt like she was beginning to accept her situation and even make the best of it.

"You can casually walk over and say hi to Destiny," Tara suggested. "Maybe she'll introduce her friend, and if it isn't Jake she's talking to, you can simply move on."

"Good idea."

I casually walked across the room, pausing to say hi to several people as I made my way toward the young couple. I was probably being ridiculous, but I didn't want to seem overly interested in Jake and scare him off. I didn't know if he was the type who would be comfortable speaking to strangers.

"Hey, Destiny," I said casually as I walked up. "Are you having fun?"

"Oh, hey, Cait. This is my friend Jake."

"I'm glad to meet you, Jake. Do you go to Destiny's school? I mean the school she used to go to?"

He nodded. "Destiny told me you're investigating Roxi Pettigrew's death. We were just talking about it."

Thank you, Destiny.

"I am. Sort of," I answered.

"Cait is really smart. She's already solved three murders this year," Destiny bragged.

I smiled at the girl I suddenly felt a ton of emotion for. She sounded so proud.

"I might know something if you're interested," Jake offered. "Destiny said I could trust you."

"I am interested. And you can trust me. Why don't we find somewhere quieter to talk?" I said. "We can go into the choir room. I don't think anyone's using it."

Destiny and Jake followed me down the hall. I turned on the light and suggested they take a seat at one of the tables. "So what did you want to share?" I asked.

"If I tell you, you have to promise not to tell anyone you got this from me," Jake began.

"I can agree to that as long as you aren't about to tell me that you did it."

Jake laughed. "No, I didn't do it. I liked Roxi, and Jimmy was really cool. I used to hang out at their apartment all the time before Jimmy died. My parents are a lot less cool."

"Okay, so what do you know?"

"Roxi was having a really hard time dealing with the situation after Jimmy died. I mean really hard. I was concerned she might commit suicide, so I started stopping by after she got home in the evenings to check on her."

I frowned.

"I know Roxi went through a marathon dating phase, but it wasn't like that between us," Jake qualified. "We were friends and I was worried about her."

"Okay. Go on."

"I stopped by maybe a month and a half ago and she had a black eye. She was hysterical. She told me some guy had come by earlier in the day and threatened to kill her if she didn't return some money that belonged to him. Roxi swore she didn't have it, that she had no idea what the guy was talking about, but he wouldn't listen. He said Jimmy owed him twenty grand and if she didn't come up with it in a few days he was going to make an example of her."

"Hawk," I said.

"That's what I told Jake," Destiny offered.

"Anyway, I managed to calm her down and told her I would help her figure out what to do. At the time we had no idea what had happened to the money if Jimmy had ever had it, so we had no way to recover it."

Jake paused. He almost looked embarrassed by what he was about to tell me. I waited quietly and let him continue.

"I guess you know Roxi found an unconventional way to raise the funds, which is what may have gotten her killed. I feel bad it came down to that, but she was scared, and she got to the point where she was willing to do anything to get this guy off her back."

"Yeah, I can understand that," I offered. "To a point."

"It did seem like her plan got the best of her. But that isn't what I wanted to talk to you about. I might know who caused Jimmy's accident."

"Really? Who?" I asked.

"A guy who lives in our complex. His name is Eric Meadowvale."

"Why do you think he might have caused Jimmy's accident?" I inquired.

"I didn't at first, but then Destiny explained about the money and the fact that the accident occurred on the way home from Jimmy's trip to Seattle. She said that if someone caused the accident to steal the money, they must have known about it. Eric knew about the duffel bags. I knew too, but I didn't kill Jimmy or steal the money. But Eric might have."

I watched as Jake wove his fingers through Destiny's. He seemed nervous about telling me what he had, and I suddenly realized he was only doing it because Destiny had asked him to. He really cared about her.

"Okay, so how do you know this Eric knew about the money?" I asked.

"Because I was there when Jimmy told him about it. Me and Eric were over at Jimmy's. I'm not sure where Roxi was, but she wasn't home. Eric and Jimmy were drinking beer and we were all watching a baseball game. Somehow we got onto the subject of money and the fact that we all needed it. Jimmy told us that he had hooked up with some guy who wanted to move some cargo, and that he was going to make a lot of money in a fairly short time. Jimmy had had a lot to drink, so he said more than he should have. Before I knew where he was going with the conversation, he was telling Eric and me all about his trips to meet the cruise ship, and how after he dropped the cargo off in Seattle someone would meet him at the ferry with a bag full of money. He didn't know how much, but he figured it was a lot. We all started shooting the breeze about what we'd do if we came in to a large sum of money. It was all in fun, until Eric started acting strange."

"Strange how?" I asked.

"He started asking a bunch of questions. Specific questions. Jimmy was so wasted he just kept spouting off about every little detail. I had a bad feeling about the whole thing. Then, a week later, Jimmy was dead. At the time I didn't realize he would have had the money in the car. Even after Roxi told me some guy was after her for the money, I didn't make the connection. Then Destiny told me tonight that he was coming back from his trip to Seattle when he had the accident, and that Deputy Finnegan thought the accident was caused by someone wanting to get to the money, and I remembered that conversation."

"Does Eric still live in your complex?" I asked.

"No. He took off after Jimmy's accident. Now I know why."

"I need to tell Finn about this."

A look of panic came across Jake's face.

"Don't worry; I'll leave your name out of it. I'll just tell Finn that I got an anonymous tip. It's possible Jimmy told other people about the money too if he told you and Eric, but it looks like we might have at least one part of this very confusing mystery solved. Thanks for trusting me with what you know."

Jake smiled at Destiny. "Destiny talked me in to it. At first I didn't want to. After all the deaths, I was scared to get involved."

"I don't blame you. I'll keep my promise not to mention your name."

I chatted with Jake and Destiny a while longer and then returned to Cody, who was knee-deep in elementary school–aged kids wanting a chance to pop a balloon with a dart. Cody was really good with them, just as he was with the choir kids. He lifted the smaller ones onto a chair to give them a better advantage and teased the teens, who really shouldn't even have been playing the game, in an attempt to mess them up. All in all, everyone seemed to be having a wonderful time.

"We're going to eat dinner in shifts," Cody informed me. "Your Aunt Maggie stopped by and said she'd send someone to relieve us in an hour or so. I just hope all the food isn't gone by then. I'm starving."

I looked around the room. It really was packed. Which was good, because it meant the ladies could buy the linens they wanted for the church.

"If the food is gone by the time we make it into the cafeteria we can grab a bite after. Have you seen where Tara ended up?"

"She's over at the bean bag toss. I saw you taking to Jake and Destiny."

"I have news. I'll fill you in later."

By the time anyone got around to relieving Cody and me, the food was mostly gone. Tara and Danny hadn't gotten a chance to eat either, so I called Finn and we headed over to O'Malley's for a burger and a beer. It looked like O'Malley's had gotten the overflow from the Harvest Festival; the place was packed. Luckily, we found a booth in the corner that was not only isolated but quiet.

Once we'd gotten our food I shared with the others what I'd found out from Jake. Finn wasn't thrilled I wouldn't reveal the name of my source, but once he could see I was adamant about not sharing that specific piece of information, he decided to respect my limitation and focus on Eric Meadowvale.

"I'll definitely track down this Eric and see what he has to say for himself," Finn promised. "I have other news as well."

We all looked at him expectantly.

"The Valdez police department tracked down Hawk, whose real name is Beverly Hawkhorn."

Everyone at the table let out a little cheer and high-fived one another.

"Hawk is a woman?" I asked.

"No, he's a man. He just had cruel parents who thought Beverly was a good name for their son. Anyway, he's in custody and is being transported to Seattle to face charges of murder, assault, and kidnapping. The kidnapping charge should stick because Danny can testify to that, and the assault charge looks good as well with Garrett's testimony, but we really don't have any proof that he killed Roxi, and now it sounds like he might not have killed Jimmy. I consider his arrest a victory nonetheless."

"And the captain of the cruise ship?" Tara asked.

"Unfortunately, he's already returned to South America. Now that he knows we're on to him, I doubt he'll come this way again."

"So we started with Roxi's murder and while we've wrapped up all the sideshows, we still haven't solved Roxi's murder," I pointed out.

"True," Finn admitted, "but in the course of following the leads into Roxi's murder we discovered Jimmy's accident might not have been an accident, and that's important. And we learned Garrett was involved with Hawk, which caused me to go out to his place, which probably saved his life, and that's important. And we were responsible for identifying a smuggling ring that was bringing drugs into our country, and that's definitely important."

"Are you sure it was drugs Hawk was smuggling?" Cody asked.

"He had one of his crates in his hotel room. It was filled with heroin."

"I still want to find Roxi's killer, but I guess we should take a minute to celebrate the fact that the coast guard found Danny in time, and Finn found Garrett in time, and a man who was bringing drugs into our country will be brought to justice." I raised my glass in a toast.

"Hear, hear," everyone chimed in as five mugs filled with O'Malley's special draft celebrated a day filled with victories both large and small.

Chapter 13

Saturday, September 26

"Here he is again," I said to Tara as the ferry pulled up to the dock.

I watched as the black and white cat strolled up. As he had every Saturday, the cat jumped up onto a bench and waited for the eleven o'clock ferry from the mainland. And, as he had every Saturday, the tall, elderly, dark-haired man wearing dark glasses and a dark suit disembarked and walked up the ramp toward the main street of Pelican Bay.

"I'm going to follow him again," I announced. "Both Cassie and Destiny are here to help you with the crowd from the ferry and I really do want to figure out what that guy is up to."

Tara must have been curious as well because she didn't argue.

"Don't lose him this time," Tara instructed.

"I won't. I'll come back to tell you what I found out before I have to head over to set up our booth for the street fair."

"Hurry," Tara counseled. "The man and the cat are already halfway down the dock and the organizer for the street fair wants all the booths set up by noon."

"I'll hurry," I promised as I left the store and began walking behind the cat who was following the man.

As he had the last time I'd followed him, the man turned the corner where the wharf met Main Street and walked briskly down the sidewalk. I followed him past Herbalities, Ship Wreck, Off the Hook, the Bait and Stitch, and For the Halibut. Two boys on bikes swerved in front of me, causing me to fall back just a bit, but I quickly righted myself and almost managed to close the gap between us when he turned the corner onto Harbor Boulevard and disappeared.

Again.

"No way," I said out loud.

I looked up and down the street, but there was absolutely no sign of the man or the cat. The only conclusion I could come to was that he was some sort of illusionist who knew how to literally disappear.

"Something wrong?" Tansy appeared behind me as if by magic.

"You're back." I hugged the woman. "How was your retreat?"

"Heavenly."

"We really need to talk about Beatrice, but for now I'd settle for figuring out how the man wearing the dark suit who I've been following seems to disappear as easily as you seem to appear. He's not a witch, is he?"

"No, not a witch."

"A warlock?"

"No. Just wait."

I stood with Tansy, silently waiting while droves of tourists gathered around us in anticipation of the opening of the street fair. I couldn't imagine what Tansy was waiting for me to see, but, with the possible exception of the defective cat she'd sent me, she'd never steered me wrong before. So I waited beside her for whatever was going to happen.

Tansy seemed content to stand serenely, looking at nothing in particular. It was times such as this that I wondered if she was even aware of the activity around her. Two kids on skateboards barreled down the street barely avoiding a collision with the two of us, yet Tansy didn't even flinch. I could feel the excitement of the crowd around us as vendors set up their booths and the scent of corn dogs, popcorn, and deep-fried onion rings filled the air.

I have to admit I'm not really good at waiting, so I found myself growing impatient just standing there for whatever was going to happen to happen.

After several minutes the man in the dark suit came out of the post office and continued down the street, followed by the black and white cat.

"He was in the post office?" I said.

Tansy just smiled.

"But the post office is closed every day from eleven to twelve thirty so Mr. Baxter can go home for lunch. He begins his day when he meets the five a.m. ferry, you know."

"Mr. Baxter waits for Sebastian to arrive on Saturdays."

"Wait? The man from the ferry has his mail delivered here?"

"Just one letter."

"But why? He doesn't even live here."

"Let's follow," Tansy suggested.

I walked beside Tansy in the direction I'd seen the man and the cat head after he left the post office. The street and sidewalks were jammed with festival visitors, so I seriously doubted my ability to find the man in the crowd, but Tansy seemed to know where we were going. We turned from Main Street onto Grove Boulevard and followed the road to the end. Located there was the Madrona Island Cemetery, on a bluff overlooking the ocean. The man with the dark glasses and dark suit was sitting on a bench beneath a tree with the black and white cat sitting next to him. Both were looking out toward the sea.

"Does the man do this every Saturday?" I asked.

"Rain or shine."

"And the cat?"

"She joins him without fail," Tansy confirmed.

I looked across the perfectly manicured lawn dotted with headstones. In spite of the fact that cemeteries in general are associated with death and horror movies in my mind, the one on Madrona Island is peaceful and serene with its huge shade trees and endless expanses of sea in the distance.

"So the man has a loved one buried in the plot near where he's sitting?"

"His wife Adeline," Tansy confirmed. "She passed away a year ago today. Just four days after the couple's sixtieth wedding anniversary."

I felt a wave of sorrow wash over me. It must be incredibly difficult to spend the majority of your life with someone only to wake up one day and realize they were gone from you forever.

"I'm sorry. It must be very difficult to lose someone who has been a part of your life for so long."

Tansy didn't say anything, but I knew she agreed with me.

"I can understand why he comes every Saturday to visit his wife's grave, but why the post office?" I asked.

"Before she passed, Adeline arranged to have a friend deliver a letter to the Madrona Island Post Office every week. There were fifty-three in all."

"Fifty-three?"

"Fifty-two of the fifty-three letters were to be delivered to the post office every Saturday beginning with the one following her death, and the fifty-third letter was to be delivered on the couple's wedding anniversary."

"Last Tuesday," I said.

"Every week Sebastian picks up the letter and has Mr. Baxter read it to him. Then he comes to the cemetery and sits with Adeline until it's time for the next ferry to leave the island for the trip east."

"Sebastian is blind," I realized.

"Yes."

"He gets around remarkably well. Especially considering that he doesn't use a cane or work with a service dog."

Tara smiled. "Sebastian has very heightened senses. His lack of eyesight doesn't hinder him in most cases."

"Except to read a letter," I murmured.

I watched as the man sat very still, never moving or adjusting his position in the least. He really did look like he was made of wax.

"Why did his wife leave him letters if she knew he couldn't read them?" I asked.

It would have made more sense for her to leave him tapes if she wanted him to have something to remember her by after she had passed.

"Adeline knew Sebastian would become so distraught when she left that he'd find it difficult to go on living."

"She was afraid he would commit suicide?"

"No, but she *was* afraid he'd simply drift away."

"Drift away?"

"Sebastian lives in a very real world that exists independently from this one. Adeline was afraid he'd choose to remain there rather than deal with the pain in this existence."

"You mean an imaginary world?"

"Not imaginary. Just not here, on this plane of existence. Adeline knew it would be important to give Sebastian a reason to maintain a hold on this reality, so she left the letters. She also wanted him to have a reason to get out of the house and to maintain contact with at least one other person."

"So she arranged for the letters to be delivered through Pete Baxter."

"Exactly. This created a situation in which Sebastian had to leave his house, take the ferry, and speak to Mr. Baxter at least once each week."

"If she left fifty-two letters and it's been a year since she died, this is the last week," I said. "Sebastian just received his last letter. Will he be okay?"

"That's for him to decide."

I thought for sure I was going to cry. I felt my heart breaking for this lonely man who had lost the only person who really mattered to him.

"Do you know what will happen to him?" I asked as a tear slid down my cheek.

Tansy shook her head. "But I do know that his time in this realm is coming to an end. Adeline will watch out for him."

"From heaven?"

"In a way."

I frowned and was about to ask her what she meant when suddenly I knew.

"The cat. Adeline is connected to the cat."

"Yes, Adeline will leave with Sebastian today when he departs on the ferry. Don't worry about the man or the cat. My sense tells me that things are as they should be."

I suddenly found myself wanting to sob. I watched as the man and the cat sat silently side by side for the last time in this particular place in time and space. Adeline had given Sebastian a wonderful gift. She'd given him the gift of herself as a bridge to help him deal with a loss she knew he would otherwise be incapable of facing. I couldn't imagine how difficult it must have been for her to write those fifty-three letters, knowing she would be gone when it came time for him to read them.

"So she knew she was going to die?"

Tansy didn't answer. I turned around. She was gone.

I never had gotten the chance to talk to Tansy about Beatrice, but suddenly I realized it didn't matter. Everything has a season, a timing, an exact moment when the realms we can experience through our senses and those we can't come together in perfect harmony, creating a symphony that reminds us that we aren't alone. I knew this was one of those moments and, like Tansy, I sensed Sebastian and Adeline would be okay.

I decided to leave the man to his final moments on the island, turned around, and headed back toward the bookstore. I was halfway down Main when Beatrice walked up beside me.

"How did you get here?"

"Meow."

"Never mind. Maybe now that Tansy's back your magical kitty powers have been ignited. Do you have something to show me?"

Beatrice began making her way through the crowd. I did my best to keep up with her, but it wasn't easy; she was small and fast and I was just small. I kept my eyes focused on the tip of her tail so I wouldn't lose her. I finally caught up to her in the park, where the chili cook-off was being held.

"Chili? Chili isn't good for cats."

Beatrice wiped her paw across her face, hiding her eyes as if to indicate that she couldn't believe how dense I was being.

"You don't want chili. You want me to see something. Or maybe speak to someone. Okay, who?"

Beatrice trotted over to a booth in the middle of the crowd, where I found Olivia Oxford speaking to Sissy Partridge. Sissy had attended the same high school I had, but she'd already graduated by the time I was a freshman.

"Afternoon, Olivia; Sissy," I greeted them. "How's the cook-off coming along?"

"It's a shoo-in to win," Olivia assured me. "Sissy has a recipe that was handed down from her great-grandmother."

"I can't wait to try it," I said politely, even though I very much doubted I'd be back to sample Sissy or anyone else's chili for that matter once tasting began. I wasn't sure what information I was supposed to get from Sissy or Olivia, so I decided to engage in idle chitchat until the subject I was here to discuss presented itself.

"Although," I added, "I do need to watch what I eat today. I'm afraid my dress for the ball tonight is already a bit too tight."

"I haven't eaten for two days," Sissy informed me. "I want to look perfect for my first social event as an engaged woman."

"You're engaged?" I hadn't even heard Sissy was dating anyone.

She held out her left hand to display a modest yet beautiful diamond solitaire. "Greg Westlake *finally* popped the question last night."

Sissy and Greg were dating? This was news to me.

"Congratulations. I wasn't aware you and Greg were seeing each other."

"The whole thing happened really fast." Sissy grinned. "I'm very excited. It seems like I've been waiting my whole life for this. To be honest, I almost gave up on my dream of being Greg's wife when he started dating Roxi, but luckily it all worked out."

I frowned. "I'm not sure I would call Roxi's death lucky, but I'm happy things worked out for you."

"Roxi was nothing more than a last fling," Olivia assured me. "It's always been Sissy Greg was destined to marry."

"I see. Well, congratulations again."

"Be sure to come back for a taste," Sissy called after me as I walked away.

"I'll try," I answered.

I looked around for Beatrice, but she was gone. I thought about looking for her, but I had no idea which direction she'd taken off in and I needed to get back to Coffee Cat Books to check in with Tara. It was after noon and I knew she was most likely stressing that I'd missed the deadline to have our booth set up.

"You're late," Tara informed me the minute I walked through the door.

"Did you hear that Greg Westlake and Sissy Partridge are engaged?"

"Engaged? I didn't even know they were dating."

"Me neither. In fact, Finn made it sound as if Greg was still pretty distraught about the whole thing with Roxi. It really doesn't make sense, unless..."

"Unless what?" Tara prompted.

"When I spoke to Olivia a week ago at the Bait and Stitch, she mentioned that Greg's mother had someone in mind for Greg once he was done sowing his wild oats. I wonder if that someone was Sissy. Maybe his mom convinced Greg to settle down with this very traditional girl she'd picked out for him after the Roxi fiasco."

"I guess I could see how that could happen," Tara commented. "Greg never has been able to stand up to his mom. I'm sure she didn't have to work too hard to convince him that making decisions for himself wasn't a good idea after Roxi used him the way she did. I hate to say it, but I doubt either Greg or Sissy will be happy in the long run."

"Yeah, I agree. Sissy mentioned she'd been waiting for Greg her whole life. Now that she has him, I wonder if she can keep him. I'd better head back to town to set up our booth. I'll have my cell. Call me if you need me."

Chapter 14

Luckily, I ran into Cody at the street fair, and he helped me set up the booth, so I wasn't really all that late. The street fair ran from noon until the ball started at eight, although I planned to shut down our booth by six so I'd have time to get ready for my big double date with Cody, Tara, and Danny.

The island was packed with tourists from the mainland who had come over on the ferry to enjoy our seasonal celebration. I did a brisk business the first three hours I was open. So brisk in fact that I had all but run out of inventory by three o'clock. I was trying to decide whether to call Tara to ask her to bring me additional items to sell or to just close down early when I saw Beatrice in the crowd.

"Can you keep an eye on my booth for a few minutes?" I asked the vendor next to me. "I see my cat has wandered downtown and I'd like to catch her before she gets into traffic."

"Certainly," the woman graciously agreed. "We wouldn't want your fur baby to get hit by a car."

"Thanks. I'll be right back."

I hurriedly walked toward where I'd last seen Beatrice. She'd moved away from that grassy area, but I quickly spotted her crossing the street. I prayed she actually wouldn't get hit by oncoming traffic, but she made her way across the busy parkway without any problem.

I followed her down Main Street toward the wharf. I tried to catch up with her, but the faster I walked the faster she ran. When she turned onto the wooden walkway leading out to the ferry I was sure she was heading for Coffee Cat Books, but she trotted right past it.

She also passed the area for ferry loading and unloading and continued onto the docks, which provided access to the boats that rented slips in the harbor. I thought she might be heading for Danny's boat, but she ran past his dock and continued on toward the last one on the end.

"Where are you going, you silly cat? There's nothing out here. Just a handful of fishing boats."

Beatrice jumped up onto the deck of the last boat on the left. I realized in an instant she'd brought me to Jimmy's boat.

"Hello," I called as I approached the vessel. I knew Roxi had sold the boat and I didn't want to just walk in on the new owner if he should be inside the cabin. "Is anyone there?" I called again.

Convinced the boat was unoccupied, I climbed aboard and then headed belowdecks to find the wandering cat.

The boat was actually fairly large. There was a full cabin that could be used to live in temporarily if one found oneself out to sea for days at a time. Beatrice was sitting on the double bunk in the only bedroom. I walked across the room to pick her up, but just as I reached for her, she jumped up onto a built-in dresser.

"Okay, what's up?" I asked. I really needed to get going. Not only did I have the ball to prepare for but I still had to take down my booth and return everything to Coffee Cat Books.

Beatrice jumped down onto the floor and began to wind herself through my legs in a circle eight pattern. She started to purr as I bent down to pick her up. Just as I was about to return to an upright position, I saw something under the bed. I got down on my knees to retrieve it and noticed the blood that was splattered on the wall behind the bed.

I picked up the item under the bed, which turned out to be a necklace, and then returned to a standing positon.

"What are you doing in here?" a voice said from behind me.

I quickly turned around. "You scared me." I put my hand to my chest. "I was just trying to catch my cat, who'd wandered aboard. What are you doing here?"

"I own this boat."

"You bought the boat from Roxi? Whatever for?"

"I made an arrangement with the whore to buy the boat in exchange for her promise to leave the island. I thought she'd leave right away, but she didn't."

I looked down at the necklace in my hand and remembered the blood on the wall. "So you killed her."

"I didn't mean to. I followed my loser of a son to the boat one day shortly after I purchased it. I saw what that woman was doing to him. Not only had she not left town as per our agreement but she was defiling my son on the boat I now owned. I'm sure it was Greg's idea. He probably thought it would be great fun to thumb his nose in my face by doing the very thing I was trying to prevent with the very woman I was trying to keep him away from. It wasn't right. My boy was meant for another. He had no right toying with that Jezebel."

"Meant for another? Sissy. You told Sissy she could marry Greg if she waited for him."

"I promised her, and I always keep my promises."

"Why? He doesn't love her."

Mrs. Westlake shrugged. "It doesn't matter. The boy will do as he's told. He always has. I came back to the boat after Greg left that afternoon. All I wanted to do was talk to the woman. Reason with her. We did after all have an agreement. But she got hysterical and told me to butt out of her personal life. She insisted that who Greg slept with was none of my business. I got mad and pushed her. She hit her head."

"Why didn't you call 911? She didn't have to die."

"I realized it was better if she did. I left, and when I came back after dark she was dead. All I needed to do was bury her in her own grave and no one would ever know. It would have worked if that idiot I got to help me had replaced the sod properly."

My eyes darted around the room as I looked for a way out. The woman was crazy. She'd just confessed to killing Roxi. There was no way she was going to simply let me go. The very wide woman stood between me and the only doorway. I had to keep her talking until I could figure out a way to get her to move.

"What idiot?" I asked.

The woman just frowned at me.

"What idiot did you get to help you?" I clarified.

She squinted her eyes and puckered her lips. "Why do you want to know?"

I shrugged. "Just curious."

I watched as the woman glared at me but didn't reply. I needed a diversion. If I could manage to slip past her, I knew without a doubt I could outrun her. She didn't appear to have a weapon, but she had to weigh three times what I did. I was pretty sure I'd be the loser in a wrestling match.

Beatrice had made her way back onto the top of the dresser while we'd been talking. I glanced at her and she glanced back. I was pretty sure we were communicating, as odd as that might sound. I nodded and she jumped off the dresser and onto Mrs. Westlake's head. The woman screamed and I ran while she was untangling herself from the cat. I paused to make sure Beatrice had escaped as well. The two of us ran as fast as we could back to Coffee Cat Books to call Finn. It looked like Beatrice had come through after all.

Chapter 15

The Masquerade Ball was a magical event at which everyone who chose to attend had the ability to pretend for one night that they lived a life much grander than the one they actually led. Most of us dressed in period clothing that represented a person in history we most wanted to emulate. Even those of us who didn't dress up as a specific personage wore formal attire that would have been appropriate at the grand balls of old.

With the craziness of the past week, Tara and I had borrowed dresses with full skirts and fitted bodices from Maggie, and Danny and Cody wore tuxes.

Cody and Danny picked Tara and me up at my cabin in a horse-drawn coach that looked like something out of a fairy tale. Between the carriage and the old-fashioned ball gown, I really felt like Cinderella. My heart pounded as Cody squeezed into the small seat next to me. I could feel my body welcome his warmth and I knew deep within my soul that I would remember every moment of this magical night for the rest of my life.

I watched in awe as the carriage pulled up in front of the white marble steps that led to the front door of the oceanfront mansion. Cody's eyes locked with mine as he put his hands around my waist and swung me into his arms. I slid slowly down his body as he set me gently on the ground. He placed my arm through his as we made our way up the steps and into the ballroom, where the orchestra was playing a beautiful waltz that had couples floating gracefully around the dance floor.

Cody led me out to join them. He placed one hand on my back while taking my hand in his. I felt like I was floating on air in a space above the marble floor as the music mixed with the magic of the night.

It turned out the ball was proving to be the perfect end to an exciting day. After the incident on the boat, Finn arrested both Greg's mother and her gardener, who had been the one she'd convinced to help her bury Roxi. The case was closed and Beatrice returned home to the people who were missing her. I don't fully understand the link between Tansy, the cats who come into my life, and my apparent role as an amateur sleuth. There are times I question whether becoming involved in these tragic occurrences is something I can continue to do, but for the time being I'll honor the responsibility that seems to have been entrusted to me.

"By the way, I forgot to tell you that I found out what that mysterious stranger was doing on the island and how he was connected to his own special cat," I said to Cody after the orchestra switched to a slightly different tempo.

"So what was his story?"

"It's really very romantic, in a sad sort of way," I began.

"That's a wonderful story," Cody said when I finished. "Sixty years with one person is truly remarkable."

"Yeah." I sighed. "Sometimes I wonder if those kinds of marriages are even possible these days. When I see how easy it seems to be for couples to betray the trust they're supposed to be committed to, it makes me lose my faith in true love. I almost feel love stories such as Sebastian's are as much a relic of the past as this ball."

Cody pulled me just a bit closer. I could feel his breath on my cheek as he spoke softly into my ear. "I believe in true love that lasts a lifetime. With the right person."

I pulled back just a bit so I could look into his eyes. "How do you know if you've found the right person? Tansy didn't say how Adeline died, but it seems she must have known she was dying. She wanted to continue to take care of Sebastian even after her death, so she used precious moments from her final days to write fifty-three letters. Fifty-three! That's the kind of love you just don't see these days."

"Your parents were married until your dad passed," Cody reminded me.

"True, but they weren't really happy. In the end they remained together because that was what the church required. Your parents divorced, and look at all the men we discovered who betrayed their wives during our investigation into Roxi's death. These are men who, prior to this investigation, I would have sworn were truly in love with their spouses. I'm sure on the day they married they believed their love would endure. But it didn't. Not like Adeline's love for Sebastian. How do you know when you've found a love that will continue to burn not only for a lifetime but beyond?"

"I don't know," Cody admitted. "Maybe love isn't *just* something you feel. Maybe it's something you do. Maybe things weren't always easy for Sebastian and Adeline. Maybe there were times when the fire of their love died to an ember. Maybe the difference is that Adeline and Sebastian made a commitment to their relationship every day of their lives, whether they felt the fire or not."

"You think so?"

"I do. I don't think marriage is a commitment you make one time on your wedding day. I think it's something you renew every moment of every day, whether it comes easily in that instant or not."

Cody and I locked eyes, and I melted into the depths of his as the orchestra segued into a slow number. While Cody and I still had miles to travel, one day I would look back on that moment and realize it was then that I made a commitment to the man I was certain I had always loved, and it was likewise then that he made a commitment to me that would endure the ups and downs of a lifetime.

Recipes for Much Ado About Felines

Recipes by Kathi:
Potato Sausage Soup
Chicken Mac and Cheese
Apple Spice Cake with Cream Cheese Frosting
Caramel Brownies

Recipes by Readers:
Cranberry Orange Scones – submitted by Robin Coxon
Pumpkin Oatmeal – submitted by Marie Rice
Seafood Salad Louis – submitted by Vivian Shane
Corn Chowder - submitted by Nancy Farris
Irish Sweet Potato Bake - submitted by Janel Flynn
Creamsicle Cake – submitted by Joyce Aiken

Potato Sausage Soup

Ingredients:

6 oz. pkg. smoked sausage links, thinly sliced (or any sausage)
4 oz. pkg. pepperoni slices
2 small onions, chopped
2 small cans sliced olives
2 cans cream of chicken soup
1 can cream of cheddar soup
2½ cups milk
1½ cups water
5 cups potatoes, peeled and cubed

Sauté sausage, pepperoni, and onion in large saucepan until meat is done and onions browned.
Drain fat. Stir in remaining ingredients.

Reduce heat and simmer until potatoes are tender.

Chicken Mac and Cheese

Ingredients:

1 box (16 oz.) penne pasta
4 chicken breasts, cooked and cubed
1 can Campbell's Cream of Cheddar soup
1 can Campbell's Nacho Cheese soup
(you can use two cans of either if you like your casserole more or less spicy)
2 cups shredded cheddar cheese
1 cup grated Parmesan cheese
1 jar (16 oz.) alfredo sauce (any brand)
¾ cup milk
1 cup cashews (or more if you'd like)
Salt and pepper to taste
Cheddar cheese crackers

Boil pasta according to directions on box (10–12 minutes).

Meanwhile, mix cooked and cubed chicken, soups, cheeses, alfredo sauce, milk, cashews, and salt and pepper together in a large bowl.

Drain pasta when tender and add to chicken mixture. Stir until well mixed.

Pour into a greased 9 x 13 baking pan. Top with crumbled cheddar cheese crackers.

Bake at 350 degrees for 30 minutes.

Apple Spice Cake with Cream Cheese Frosting

Ingredients for cake:

1½ cups all-purpose flour
1½ tsp. cinnamon
1 tsp. baking soda
¾ tsp. salt
3 large apples, peeled and grated
1½ cups sugar
2 large eggs, beaten
½ cup vegetable oil

Mix together flour through salt. In a bowl mix apples and sugar. Add to flour mixture. Add eggs and oil.

Bake at 350 degrees in greased and floured pan (one 9 x 13 or two round cake pans) for 25–30 minutes. Let cool.

Frosting:

¾ cup butter, softened
6 oz. cream cheese, softened
1 tbs. vanilla
3 cups powdered sugar

Whip together and frost cake when cool; top with pecans.

Caramel Brownies

Ingredients:

Layer 1:

1 cup butter, softened
2 cups sugar
4 eggs
1 tsp. vanilla
½ tsp. salt
½ cup unsweetened cocoa powder
1⅓ cup flour

Layer 2:

1 (10 oz.) box vanilla wafers
6 oz. cream cheese, softened
½ cup sugar
14 oz. bag caramel cubes, unwrapped
2 tbs. milk
1½ cups milk chocolate chips
½ cup semi-sweet milk chocolate chips
1 tbs. shortening

Preheat oven to 350 degrees.

Layer 1

Cream butter and sugar together in a large mixing bowl. Add vanilla and eggs and mix well. Add salt, cocoa powder, and flour and stir to combine well. Do not overmix.
Pour into a greased 9 x 13–inch pan.
Bake at 350 degrees for 22–25 minutes.

Layer 2
Place cookies in a food processor until fine powder. If you don't have a food processor it's okay to use graham cracker crumbs.
Mash in cream cheese and sugar until mixture is well combined.
Gently press over cooled brownies.

Layer 3:
Place caramel cubes and milk in a medium microwave-safe bowl. Microwave in 30-second increments until melted, stirring in between each increment until melted and smooth.
Evenly pour over layer 2.
Place in fridge to let it cool.

Layer 4:
Combine chocolate chips and shortening together in a medium microwave-safe bowl. Microwave in 30-second increments, stirring in between each increment until melted and smooth.

Evenly spread over the top of cooled caramel layer.

Let set in fridge before cutting into.

Cranberry Orange Scones

Submitted by Robin Coxon

I love to visit a coffee shop that offers scones, but especially cranberry orange scones with orange butter.

Ingredients:

1 cup dried cranberries
¼ cup orange juice
2 cups flour
10 tsp. granulated sugar, divided (7 tsp., 3 tsp.)
1 tbs. orange peel
2 tsp. baking powder
½ tsp. salt
¼ tsp. baking soda
½ cup cold butter

¼ cup half and half (or cream)
1 tsp. vanilla
1 egg
1 tbs. milk

Glaze:

½ cup confectioner's sugar
½ tsp. vanilla
1 tbs. orange juice

Orange butter:
½ cup butter, softened
2–3 tbs. orange marmalade

Preheat oven to 400 degrees.

In a small bowl soak dried cranberries in ¼ cup orange juice. Set aside.

In a large bowl combine flour, 7 tsp. sugar, orange peel, baking powder, salt, and baking soda, and stir until mixed.

Cut cold butter into flour mixture until coarse crumbles form.

In the small bowl that holds the dried cranberries and orange juice add half and half (cream), vanilla, and egg. Stir until blended.

Add small bowl of ingredients to large bowl with flour mixture. Stir until combined.

Dump out mixture onto floured surface and gently knead 6–8 times. Pat into 8-inch circle. Cut into 8–10 wedges.

Place on ungreased cookie sheet but do not let them touch each other. Brush with 1 tbs. milk and sprinkle with remaining 3 tsp. of sugar.

Bake 12–15 minutes until golden brown. Remove from cookie sheet and let cool on wire rack.

Mix the ingredients for glaze and drizzle on cooled scones.

Mix ingredients for orange butter and serve with scones.

Scones are good without orange butter too.

Pumpkin Oatmeal

Submitted by Marie Rice

In the winter of 2012–13, I went through a hot oatmeal phase and began working on this flavoring but got interrupted and didn't get it tweaked until the autumn of 2014. Because the plain oatmeal was just too bland and I was trying to cut down on the total sugar, I would add if I just added sugar to sweeten the oatmeal, this is one of the versions that I came up with. I use unsweetened apple juice, but regular apple juice is good too. The raisins add a little sweetness (especially when using unsweetened juice) and also provide a good source of dietary iron.

Ingredients:

⅓ cup old-fashioned oats (or ¼ cup fine-milled Scottish oatmeal)
½ tsp. pumpkin pie spice
2 tbs. (approx.) dark raisins (I just eyeball it and pour some into my bowl)
2 tbs. canned or fresh pumpkin (not pie filling)
¾ cup apple juice or apple cider
⅛ tsp. vanilla extract

Place ingredients in order specified into a microwavable bowl. Sprinkle on the spice and raisins and then stir in the juice. Microwave for 1½ minutes and stir. Microwave for another 30 seconds and then continue microwaving in 15-second increments until desired consistency is achieved. Stir once again and enjoy.

Notes:

If the extract taste is too strong, don't fill the measuring spoon all the way, or use a dropper to better control the amount you want.

If additional sweetness is required, add a little honey or agave syrup after microwaving is complete.

Seafood Salad Louis

Submitted by Vivian Shane

Crabbing is one of the simple joys of living in the Pacific Northwest. I love to make this salad when we have a successful catch of fresh Dungeness crab! This recipe serves two, so adjust the ingredient amounts accordingly if you're serving more guests.

Ingredients:

1½ cups uncooked rotini (spiral pasta)
⅓ cup mayonnaise or salad dressing
2 tbs. chopped green onions
3 tbs. chili sauce
1 tsp. lemon juice
¼ lb. fresh or frozen medium shrimp, shelled, deveined, cooked, and thawed
¼ lb. fresh or frozen crabmeat, cooked, thawed, and flaked
2–4 leaves leaf lettuce
Garnish with tomato and hard-boiled egg wedges

Cook rotini per package directions. While pasta is cooking, combine mayo, green onions, chili sauce, and lemon juice in a medium bowl and mix well. Drain pasta and rinse with cold water until cool. Add rotini, shrimp, and crab to mayo mixture in the bowl and toss gently to mix. Serve on lettuce-lined plates.

Corn Chowder

Contributed by Nancy Farris

Growing up in the corn belt in Ohio, corn found its way into all food categories. If you want it to be vegetarian, substitute the bacon with olive oil. Did I mention that I always serve it with cast-iron corn bread?

Ingredients:

2 stalks chopped celery
½ cup chopped onion
2 slices chopped bacon or 2 tbs. olive oil
1 can (15½ oz.) whole kernel corn, drained
1 can (15½ oz.) creamed corn, undrained
2 cups chicken broth
2 cups milk
½ cup heavy cream
3 dashes hot sauce
2 cups cubed potatoes
2 tbs. butter, softened
2 tbs. flour
Salt and freshly ground pepper

Cook celery, onion, and bacon over medium heat for 5–10 minutes until tender, stirring occasionally.

Add both corns, broth, milk, cream, and hot sauce. Bring to boil, then reduce heat to simmer. Cover and simmer for 20 minutes.

Add potatoes, return to boil, reduce heat to simmer, cover, and cook for 15 minutes or until potatoes are tender.

In a small bowl combine butter and flour, then stir until smooth. Add to soup mixture, stirring until thickened and bubbling. Cook and stir for another minute or two.

Season with salt and pepper to taste. Top with chopped parsley if desired.

Irish Sweet Potato Bake

Submitted by Janel Flynn

Ingredients:

8 cups sweet potatoes, peeled and sliced very thin
6 tbs. butter
½ cup brown sugar
½ cup flour
2 cups heavy cream
1 cup milk

Preheat oven to 350 degrees.

Place potatoes in 3–4–quart casserole. In saucepan melt butter, stir in brown sugar until dissolved. Stir in flour, then gradually add cream and milk. Bring to a boil over medium heat until thickened. Pour sauce over potatoes. Place casserole on a cookie sheet and cook covered at 350 degrees for 1 hour. Remove cover and cook for another 30 minutes. Remove from oven.

Creamsicle Cake

Submitted by Joyce Aiken

My neighbor gave me this recipe about thirty years ago because she knew my husband loved Creamsicles.

Ingredients:

1 box orange or yellow cake mix
2 3-oz. pkg. orange Jell-O
1 cup milk
1 3-oz. pkg. instant vanilla pudding
1 8-oz. container Cool Whip

Prepare 1 box orange or yellow cake mix as directed in a 9 x 13 pan. Cool cake. Poke cake full of holes with a fork.

Mix 1 3-oz. box orange Jell-O, 1 cup boiling water, and ½ cup cold water. Stir thoroughly.
Pour over cake. Refrigerate for a half hour.

Mix by hand 1 cup milk and the vanilla instant pudding. Fold in the second package of orange Jell-O (just the dry powder) and the Cool Whip. Spread over the cake.

Refrigerate at least two hours before serving.

Books by Kathi Daley

Come for the murder, stay for the romance.

Buy them on Amazon today.

Zoe Donovan Cozy Mystery:

Halloween Hijinks
The Trouble With Turkeys
Christmas Crazy
Cupid's Curse
Big Bunny Bump-off
Beach Blanket Barbie
Maui Madness
Derby Divas
Haunted Hamlet
Turkeys, Tuxes, and Tabbies
Christmas Cozy
Alaskan Alliance
Matrimony Meltdown
Soul Surrender
Heavenly Honeymoon

Hopscotch Homicide
Ghostly Graveyard - *October 2015*
Santa Sleuth - *December 2015*

Paradise Lake Cozy Mystery:

Pumpkins in Paradise
Snowmen in Paradise
Bikinis in Paradise
Christmas in Paradise
Puppies in Paradise
Halloween in Paradise – *August 2015*

Whales and Tails Cozy Mystery:

Romeow and Juliet
The Mad Catter
Grimm's Furry Tail
Much Ado About Felines
Legend of Tabby Hollow – *September 2015*
Cat of Christmas Past – *November 2015*

Seacliff High Mystery:

The Secret
The Curse
The Relic
The Conspiracy – *October 2015*

Road to Christmas Romance:

Road to Christmas Past

Kathi Daley lives with her husband, kids, grandkids, and Bernese mountain dogs in beautiful Lake Tahoe. When she isn't writing, she likes to read (preferably at the beach or by the fire), cook (preferably something with chocolate or cheese), and garden (planting and planning, not weeding). She also enjoys spending time on the water when she's not hiking, biking, or snowshoeing the miles of desolate trails surrounding her home.

Kathi uses the mountain setting in which she lives, along with the animals (wild and domestic) that share her home, as inspiration for her cozy mysteries.

Stay up to date with her newsletter, *The Daley Weekly*. There's a link to sign up on both her Facebook page and her website, or you can access the sign-in sheet at: **http://eepurl.com/NRPDf**

Visit Kathi:

Facebook at Kathi Daley Books, **www.facebook.com/kathidaleybooks**

Kathi Daley Teen –
www.facebook.com/kathidaleyteen

Kathi Daley Books Group Page –
https://www.facebook.com/groups/569578823146850/

Kathi Daley Books Birthday Club- get a book on your birthday -
https://www.facebook.com/groups/1040638412628912/

Kathi Daley Recipe Exchange -
https://www.facebook.com/groups/752806778126428/

Webpage - **www.kathidaley.com**

E-mail - **kathidaley@kathidaley.com**

Recipe Submission E-mail –
kathidaleyrecipes@kathidaley.com

Goodreads:
https://www.goodreads.com/author/show/7278377.Kathi_Daley

Twitter at Kathi Daley@kathidaley -
https://twitter.com/kathidaley

Tumblr -
http://kathidaleybooks.tumblr.com/

Amazon Author Page -
http://www.amazon.com/Kathi-Daley/e/B00F3BOX4K/ref=sr_tc_2_0?qid=1418237358&sr=8-2-ent

Pinterest -
http://www.pinterest.com/kathidaley/

Made in the USA
San Bernardino, CA
06 April 2018